KARI KILGORE

Four-Legged Heroes

WHEN PETS RESCUE PEOPLE

Spiral Publishing, Ltd.

Dogs Know the Human Heart
George brings his newly rescued dog in for a
checkup. Hoping Dr. Joanne gives Sunny the all-
clear.
Joanne loves meeting pets and people. Especially
those getting a fresh start.
Sparks fly between them with Sunny's cheerful
help.

An Open Window to Love, or Danger?
A young woman finds a surprise after a long,
hard day.
A new roommate in the form of a gorgeous
calico cat.
The best friend she never knew she needed until
then.
But cats know best when it comes to humans, good
or bad.

Setting a Sweet Example
Blue from too many hard changes, Clara invites two
new dogs into her life.
Sweet girls rescued from a rough start, hoping for a
safe place to land.
But her best friend suspects Clara needs the safe
place even more.

An Unlikely Ally

Hildar treasures his solitary rainy season
adventures.

Exploring the desert city of Profant while everyone
else hides indoors.

Wandering hidden parts of his father's house most
never see.

Then an unusual and wonderful creature surprises
him in a forbidden passageway.

Popcorn Knows Treasure When She Sees It

Amber looks forward to visiting her favorite antique
shop, only to find unexpected change.

Kirstie settles in to her new business, hoping to
make friends.

Hard work in a small town.

All while one smart kitty makes her own plans.

The Changes Cascade

Near Future Forward (with Jason A. Adams)

Dispatches from the Galaxy: A Space Opera Novella Trio

Dangerous Days on a Pleasure Planet

Storms of Future Past:

Dreaming the Storm

Joining the Storm

Into the Storm

Fighting the Storm

Storms of the Heart

Storms of Future Past Omnibus

Voices Through Time:

Songs in the Mountain

Secrets in the Land

Sorrows in the Earth

Walking the Ghosts

The Odd Society:

Independent by Means of Magic

Protected by Means of Magic

Collections:

Fantastic Shorts: Volume 1

Fantastic Shorts: Volume 2

Fantastic Shorts: Volume 3

Escape into Romance

Stepping Out of Reality

Facing Down Extraordinary

Hacking Cybercrime

Investigations Beyond Belief

Passages in the Real World

Fantastic Side Trips

A Kaleidoscope of Cat Tales

A Tapestry of Holiday Tales

Aunties Among Us

Anthologies *with Jason A. Adams*:

Partners in Romance

Shadows Mountain Deep

Uncommon Holidays

Partnership in Crime

CONTENTS

THE JOYS OF ANIMALS SHARING OUR LIVES

Those of us lucky enough to have been owned by pets understand how much they bring to our lives.

Companionship, entertainment, and with most (but not all) companion animals, a warm snuggle on a chilly night. They help get us out into the world in many cases, often introducing us to new friends.

They can protect us in more ways than one, though I'm of the firm belief that my job is to keep *them* safe, not the other way around. Their protection can mean everything from alerting us to something wrong in our surroundings or providing an excellent evaluation of people in our lives.

And sometimes, if we're truly fortunate, they help us understand ourselves well enough to make positive changes in our lives.

I've been incredibly privileged to have known many wonderful animals over the years, and I hope to continue that good fortune for the rest of my days.

My family had a fish tank in the 1970s, and I later shared my room with a hamster named Dottie. She was a remarkably talented escape artist who always got herself caught by climbing up curtains. We had two wonderful dogs as well, Lady and Tramp, who confirmed my suspicion that I was a dog person at heart.

The 1980s brought guinea pigs and a delightful mouse named Milo. That was also the decade I moved out on my own and took in my first rescue dog. A German Shepherd/Labrador/Great Dane mix who ended up with the rather silly name Golly.

The thing about Golly was how incredibly smart she was. She swiped a partly eaten lasagna off the kitchen counter and carefully tucked the empty pan under the couch before anyone got home. Once when she had an upset tummy, she buried the result under freshly washed clothing. I was too impressed with her rather clever response to get upset, of course.

And the one that impressed me most was another time when she'd again had an accident, which was thankfully much easier to clean up than the one she buried.

We'd rescued another sweetheart of a dog named Bonzo by then, and he had the odd habit of walking in a circle when he relieved himself. The night of Golly's accident, she imitated that pattern with the evidence inside, then pretended to go when we took her out. It was only because I happened to notice she was faking by the light of a passing car that her poor best friend Bonzo avoided getting scolded.

I know, that all could easily be coincidence, or natural behavior. But even all these years later, I've never come across a dog as smart as Golly was. Thankfully she was patient enough with me to teach my then-inexperienced self how to be a pet parent.

And she was my introduction to what amazing judges of people animals can be. Despite my not believing her in a couple of cases at first, Golly was never once wrong about who I should trust, and who I shouldn't.

She was immediately smitten with my then-boyfriend Jason A. Adams, and yes, her enthusiastic endorsement played a role in the two of us getting married way back in the early 1990s.

We did rescue a shy and amazingly brave Pit Bull mix named Bella years later who decided to never trust anyone besides me or Jason after her particularly rough start in life, so that rule doesn't *always* apply.

Over the years we've rescued several cats as well, including one named Lorelei who you'll meet in this collection. She basically walked herself into our apartment and made it clear she was there to stay.

I loved all of them, but one special kitty with long, silky black hair named Loretta turned me into a true cat person about ten years ago.

That's the thing about welcoming pets as part of your life. Different as they might be, they all add their own unique type of love and joy and education, no matter their species.

There are too many others to name, but I will say a little bit more about our newest rescue dogs, Pebbles the Pibble and Great Dana, who you'll also meet in these pages and in tales to come.

That's another great thing about pets. They give writers endless inspiration and rarely get upset at how we describe them in stories.

After losing Bella and our sweet redbone hound boy Gosamer a few years ago, we hadn't made specific plans to bring in dogs. But Pebbles and Dana had their own timetable as rescue critters so often do.

We've never actually set out to get a dog. They deliver themselves.

Dana and Pebbles had impeccable timing, as has always been the case with such things.

And even after all the wonderful critters I've been lucky enough to love and have as part of my life, I've never seen dogs so closely bonded as these two. They play together, snuggle together, fuss and quarrel, and depend on each other constantly.

As long as they each know where the other one is, all is well.

Even after coming through a rough start and difficult situations, they're still excited and happy and overjoyed with every new day. Something many humans, including me, can use frequent reminders of in these early years of the 2020s.

That's one of the best lessons we can learn from our pets, especially rescues. They may not have had a standard beginning, and they've too often ended up down on their luck in some way. But they have such gratitude for their changed circumstances, and they never seem to suffer from a lack of love to share around.

One of my favorite t-shirts says "Rescued Is My Favorite Breed," and I love hearing about how much rescued animals have brought to people's lives when I wear it. And of course I don't mind one bit when folks ask me about my own rescued critters.

That's one reason I wanted to go with a theme of animals rescuing people for this genre-spanning collection. The rescues in my life have given so much more than they received, and the pets in these stories do as well.

The Best Judge of Human Character is set in my frequently visited fictional town of Lightning

Gap, Virginia. It's a standalone story that follows a short story I wrote last year called *Sunny with a Chance of Happiness*. In that story, new empty nester George rescues Sunny when he needs a bit of joy in his life. This sweet romantic story finds Sunny returning the favor.

Genre and mood shift for *The Siren's Yowl*, and the pet in question changes to the feline variety. A lonely, workaholic young attorney comes home to discover a calico cat perched on her kitchen table. As is so often the case, the human narrator gains much more than she expects by taking in a sweet stray.

Another of my typical shifts in genre brings us to *The Storms That Save You*, set in my epic fantasy series Misfortune and Magic. In the forthcoming novels, Hildar is an adult who's fallen on difficult times himself. This story finds him as a boy enjoying the pleasure of a rare rainy day in his desert city. The actions of a delightful creature called a *slemich* drive change in several lives.

The Part That Loves the Most returns to the here-and-now, with Clara struggling to adjust to a series of difficult changes in her life. A pair of energetic, affectionate young dogs who bear a striking resemblance to our recent rescues help bring joy and a new perspective.

And finally, *Popcorn and the Precious Pebbles Antique Shop* visits a town full of those wonderful stores that have become rare in the era of online selling and auction sites. A sprawling, fascinating antique shop where the items inside aren't garbage that would be better off in a landfill, but simply beloved possessions in holding before they begin their new lives. Popcorn the cat proves herself an expert in discovering treasure of all kinds.

Before anyone asks, real-life pet names do indeed help inspire fictional place names.

I hope you enjoy meeting these wonderful critters—and the humans lucky enough to welcome them into their lives—as much as I enjoyed writing the stories. Perhaps you'll be reading with a cat or dog close by, or by the light of a soothing fish tank, or with a cherished animal companion of another kind. Or maybe you share your life with beloved turtles, rats, snakes, iguanas, spiders, horses, sheep, birds, frogs, or other well-cared-for friends.

If you're fortunate enough to discover a *slemich* or another friendly fantasy creature, I certainly hope you'll let me in on the secret.

I often share photos of my own pets as part of my irregular newsletter inside The Confidential Adventure Club, and I love to see the critters readers share their lives with.

If you want to keep up with what I'm doing next, get free stories and access to exclusive ebooks and print versions not available anywhere else, and find out about Kickstarters and other fun projects, head over to www.ConfidentialAdventureClub.com.

Hope to see you there!

For more stories where speculative elements are slight or not there at all, visit www.KariKilgore.com/ContemporaryFiction.

You'll discover more fantasy of many kinds at www.KariKilgore.com/Fantasy.

For more visits to the Appalachian Mountains in and around Virginia, head on over to www.KariKilgore.com/TalesfromAppalachia.

You can also check out www.KariKilgore.com to learn more about me and find other short stories, along with novellas, novels, and more collections.

And last but certainly not least, thank you for your support of me and my writing. It means the world to me and keeps me coming back to tell the next tale.

March 2022

Four-Legged Heroes

KARI KILGORE
AUTHOR OF ODDS AND ENDINGS AND THE EARWORMS
The Best Judge of Human Character
A Lightning Gap Story

For all the furry matchmakers

1

GEORGE EDWARDS COULDN'T REMEMBER the last time he stepped into the veterinarian's office in Lightning Gap. Probably not since his kids were small enough to carry on his shoulders, and both of them were enjoying their first week of college on this fine September morning.

Long enough ago that on first glance, he felt like every single thing inside the converted Victorian on Lightning Rock Road had changed.

Well, maybe not *every*thing. Like so many businesses tucked into the colorful grand old homes, whoever handled the original conversion back before George was born did a great job of blending the classic and modern touches.

The finish on the original century-old hardwood floor was built up thick enough to withstand whatever ailing or anxious critters might throw at it, and subtly textured to cut down on slips and slides. But the beautiful grain and rich colors of oak still shone through.

Mostly hidden rows of recessed lighting kept the broad lobby bright and cheerful, while the groovy Art Deco overhead lights and wall sconces brought stylish flair no modern building could hope to match.

George didn't catch the same reliable and pleasant aromas as he did in other converted Victorians around town, not that he detected any offensive stink one might expect from a vet's office and animal hospital with boarding runs out back. Rather than the lovely scents of old books and Earl Gray tea at the Odds and Endings bookstore, or the heady rush of strong coffee and comfort food at Kay's Café, the lobby only smelled of citrus and some kind of pleasant, earthy scent he couldn't quite place.

He remembered that the closed door to his left led to the groomer's room, and he could see several more closed doors down the long hallway straight ahead, but no signs of movement. George glanced at his smartphone, even though verifying the time had passed the vet's nine o'clock opening hour seemed silly.

He and his brand new four-legged friend had just walked through the door, after all.

A couple of irritated feline voices and energetic barks let him know the building wasn't entirely deserted even though the lobby was empty so far. He wasn't quite impatient enough to call out or ring the old-fashioned brass bell that still sat front and center on the dark wooden check-in desk no matter how many things had changed around it.

There certainly hadn't been not one but three sleek flat-screen monitors on the check-in desk during George's past visits, though he did recall a bulky white one that had to top forty pounds taking up most of the space. No one back then needed anything resembling the Wi-Fi password that scrolled past on a rectangular screen on the wall that reminded him of the firehose of doom along the bottom of cable news channels.

He was pretty sure he would have remembered a touch-screen on the wall beside the groomer's office with little mini-courses on the anatomy of dogs, cats, horses, and even cows. But he did know his kids would have loved that back when they were bringing in their various birds and mice and fish.

Everything George's wife Lacy could manage to be around without falling into one of her epic sneezing fits. She'd never even walked into this office to make the attempt at tending to tiny pet illnesses, her allergies were so dreadful.

Then her own illness had carried her away from all of them fifteen long years ago.

So George stood in a time-warp daze, not holding either of his kid's hands anymore.

Today he held a rope that was a sorry substitute for a leash, leading a grinning white dog with an adorable collection of black spots attached to the other end. Two floppy triangular ears set off a broad, blocky head that somehow matched her lean pointer body.

And when she tilted her head just right—like she was right now at a particularly indignant kitty yowl from the back—her black ear stood itself up like the world's cutest pirate flag.

Sunny had appeared out of the woods only an hour or so ago, surprising George out of his freshly-emptied-nest funk. She'd made it clear from the first cautious ear skritches that she intended for George to take care of her.

He already suspected that little equation would actually work the other way around.

George reached down and ran his hand along her back, getting a wriggling tail wag in return.

"Sounds like someone's back there, huh girl? Maybe we should ring that bell after all. I bet you'd tilt your head like crazy at the big old chime it makes."

Sunny gazed up at him with huge brown eyes that had already lost a good bit of their wariness. She licked his hand, then shook herself with enough energy to send her ears flapping and a little cloud of white hairs drifting around her.

She focused on the long hallway then, with the whole-body-freeze intensity of her hunting dog ancestry shining through. After a few seconds of staring, she let out a low growling bark, only the second one George had heard.

But she showed no signs of worry or fear. In fact, she pushed back with her front legs outstretched, backside in the air, and tail waving.

About as clear a sign of relaxation and eagerness to play as George had ever seen.

"Well *hello* there, cutie," a woman said, sending George's own head snapping toward the hall.

The person walking toward him was most definitely *not* the same kindly older man he remembered, always making sure to answer all his children's questions no matter how many or how detailed the answers turned out to be.

Rather than varying shades of blue scrubs and short hair that had gotten increasingly gray and sparse over time, she had a thick fall of wavy red tresses, and wore agreeably scuffed and faded jeans. Only her short white jacket and warm smile were the same, to the point that he wondered if the previous veterinarian was a relative.

"Dr. Robinette, I presume?" George said, stepping forward with Sunny in wiggling lockstep beside him. "Sorry to just walk in here without calling so early in the day."

"Now why on earth would you apologize for bringing in such a pretty girl as this?" She paused long enough to let Sunny sniff both hands, her knees, and her shoes, then pop back up for a quick kiss of her knuckles before looking at George from his same height. "And a real *sweetheart* on top of that. I'm Joanne Robinette."

George blinked at the happy little flip in his belly as her bright green eyes met his, and somehow kept himself from a surprised gasp at the repeat performance when her hand took his in a warm, firm grip.

"George Edwards," he managed to say once he got a good breath into his lungs. "And this bundle of joy right here is Sunny."

"I'd say that's just about a perfect name for a new best friend who shows up with the dawn."

He must not have had his expression nearly as under control as he thought, because Dr. Robinette let out a deep, smooth laugh and touched his arm, setting off another of those internal gyrations.

His belly was every bit as energetic as Sunny this morning for some reason.

"I'm sorry," she said, "that probably sounds like I've been stalking you or something equally nefarious. This probably won't surprise you since you've lived in Lightning Gap your whole life, but I had a couple of calls before you and Sunny arrived. You might say the grapevine is all fired up over your new family member."

"Let me guess. One was my gossipy sister Sophie. And the other was at least one of the almost as gossipy but much sweeter Seagons. Either way, I'm glad you were expecting us, Dr. Robinette."

She waved one long-fingered hand at him and smiled, then knelt in front of Sunny. Who promptly took several bouncy steps backward, apparently so she could dance herself forward into her new veterinarian's arms.

"From what your sister said, who is indeed rather chatty every time she stops by, you knew my uncle Johnny Anderson when he was the vet here. So you're too close to my age to not call me Joanne."

George couldn't help watching those hands again while Sunny nearly smacked her own head with her wagging tail. Even though she was muttering sweet nothings that had Sunny grunting and panting with joy, Joanne was gently examining her furry body.

Brushing her fingertips along the contours of Sunny's face, then along the sides of her neck and down to her chest. Continuing on to her back, ribs, chest, and belly.

All while Sunny absolutely ate up the attention

and affection with no clue that she was actually getting checked over at A Doctor's Office.

George was equally fascinated, and wishing he'd come across a human doctor who could have managed that little trick with his kids when they were young and fussy.

"Okay, I'll do my best with that, Joanne. You've got a neat trick of checking her over without her noticing."

She grinned up at him, and George was alarmed to feel his face heating a bit with yet another belly jump.

He'd never claimed to be immune to women after losing Lacy, not at all. He'd simply been too busy raising two rambunctious twins and working in his father's tree removal and maintenance business to have a spare minute to think about romance.

And with kids in college now, and his chattery sister working in the tree business, *and* all three of them not missing any chance to suggest he really should think about dipping a toe into the world of dating over the last few weeks...

He was slowly realizing now might be the time.

"Don't worry," Joanne said, scrubbing Sunny's back and getting a shower of kissies all around her chin as a reward. "Once we get her back to an exam room and switch to things that aren't quite as easily disguised, she'll understand where she is. Assuming she's ever been to a vet's office before."

Now George's belly flopped in an altogether more unpleasant way.

"You didn't find anything wrong, did you?"

Joanne shook her head and touched his arm again as she stood, and the pleasant little flutter found its way to his heart.

"Not a thing from what I can tell. Sunny seems to be about a year old, and I'd say she's in great health pending a couple of other tests. She looks wonderful, truly, to go along with such a sweet temperament. Want me to really check her out for you?"

George wanted to ask whether she had time, which he knew was absurd since no one else had yet walked into the lobby with an ailing dog, cat, hamster, or perhaps a snake.

He'd developed what Sophie called an annoying habit of stepping to the side over the last few years. One she thought it was high time he got over.

Another look at Joanne's smile—and the adoring way Sunny gazed up at her—made him think his dratted sister might be right in this case.

"That would be fantastic if you can," he said. "And Mr. Seagon said they called around to see whether anyone reported her missing, but it might be good if you have somewhere you can check too."

Joanne nodded toward the hallway.

"Come on back then, first door on the right. You're not having second thoughts?"

"No, not at all. No time for thoughts at all between Sunny, Sophie, Mr. Seagon, and my kids. Don't get me wrong, she really is a sweetheart, and she's got a home if she wants one. I just want to make sure someone else isn't missing her, you know?"

After opening a door painted bright blue with *Exam Room One* in bold white script, Joanne stared at him for a few seconds. The shiver in his middle made a return, but he was sure he saw a little uncertainty in her eyes.

A lot like the way Sunny had regarded him that morning after she appeared out of the woods.

He could just about hear Joanne wondering if he was going to be a *nice* human, too.

"I do know," she said. "You don't want to get attached if there's no chance she can stay. I'll ask around to make sure, but I haven't heard a word about anyone losing this sweetheart. And I'm sure they would have. Okay?"

George smiled and nodded, following Sunny into the bright yellow exam room.

Those words sounded more true than he wanted to admit.

And he hoped meeting Sunny wouldn't turn out to be the only pleasant surprise of the day.

2

JOANNE STEPPED into the exam room after George and Sunny and closed the door, wondering if she'd let herself get hopelessly out of practice in reading humans.

Animals were so, *so* much easier, even though they couldn't point to where it hurt or explain it in words.

They might be able to try to cover things up, but none she'd ever met had the ability to decide to lie cruelly like people could. Or to only pretend to be interested, or loyal, or kind.

She took a minute to wash her hands at a tiny steel sink set into a short bit of blue countertop that served as workspace and landing pad for samples and vaccinations and such, trying to catch hold of her galloping heart before it could jump to too many conclusions and get her into trouble.

Then when she turned around and got another good look at handsome George Edwards, with his friendly face and fantastic head full of black curls, her stomach and even her mind joined in the nonsense. Right then he sat in one of the easy-clean tan chairs tucked alongside the wall, scratching Sunny's long, sturdy neck, watching her tilt this way and that to direct his hand.

His heart-melting smile and the adoration plain in his warm green eyes threw her entirely off her habitual new-pet-intake procedure for several wonderful seconds that she didn't regret one little bit.

No matter how the next half hour or so went, this one could turn out to be trouble.

The guy, not the pup.

"Okay, this next bit can be a bit uncomfortable for the critters and the new critter guardians," she said. "But I think we'll get through just fine. Ready to step up for me, Sunny girl?"

Sunny looked confused for a moment, switching her stare from Joanne to the silvery hydraulic-lift exam table set to its lowest position in the middle of the room. Joanne bent over and tapped it a couple of times with her fingernails, but Sunny only tilted her head to the side and continued to look like an adorable goofball.

Then she turned to George with her ears raised and tufts of eyebrow whiskers perked forward. She couldn't have said "A little help here?" more clearly if she'd been able to speak English.

George stood and clicked his tongue, pointing to the table as if he'd brought dogs in for exams once a month for years.

"Pop up here and let Dr. Joanne check you out."

Sunny sniffed the edge of the table, nose traveling around the edge in both directions, before she stepped up. Her flipped-back ears and low-sweeping tail made it clear she wasn't quite sure about all this, but okay.

"She's young enough that we're not worried about too many things," Joanne said, "but I'll check her temperature to make sure. Then if it's all right with both of you, I'll draw a little blood to test for parasites. I'm afraid I'll need to check her poo for that as well, which most dogs like almost as well as getting their temperatures taken."

George laughed, and the joyful sound of it echoed inside Joanne's heart and mind like an agreeable jolt of heat lightning.

"I haven't made a trip to this office for a long time, but I remember exactly how my kids felt about getting those kinds of checkups. Can't say I've known Sunny for long enough to be sure, but I get the feeling she'll react better than they did. Did you take over from your uncle?"

He positioned himself in front of Sunny, rubbing her blocky white head and looking into her eyes, before Joanne needed to suggest it. Thankfully Sunny was big enough to reach the necessary parts without putting her through lifting the table on her very first visit.

"Not directly. He had a younger buddy of his from vet school step in while I was finishing up my training. I've been working up here for a couple of years, but only moved to Lightning Gap over the summer. Sorry about this, Sunny, it will only take a second. Sophie tells me your kids just started college."

With only a couple of startled glances from Sunny and plenty of reassurance from George, the most undignified parts went quickly.

This time George's smile was proud and only a little bit wistful.

"They did, one in Atlanta and one in Nashville. They demanded photos of their new little sister as soon as Sophie scooped me on announcing Sunny's arrival. So word pretty much got out before I even had time to get back to my truck after I spoke to Mr. Seagon."

"That's right, you and Sunny have already gotten the Odds and Endings magic treatment. Mrs. Seagon says they sent you on your way with a couple of books, which is no surprise to anyone who's ever set foot in the best bookstore in the world."

As was so often the case, Sunny didn't mind the

quick blood draw nearly so much as the earlier attention paid to her hindquarters.

George flashed a shy glance Joanne's way, one that only turned up the curiosity and fascination taking over the part of her brain that wasn't focused on Sunny. Who was currently tolerating a stethoscope held in several places around her chest with only a series of curious sniffs.

He might be a new dog guardian, but George didn't say a word until Joanne was finished listening in to Sunny's calm breathing and strong heartbeat.

"Yeah, Mr. Seagon gave me a book about taking care of dogs, which I'll absolutely need. And another all about how pets rescue people. I think Sunny already has designs on that, but I'm looking forward to reading it."

"I've always said pets do more for us than we could ever do for them." She hesitated for a second, wondering how bold she wanted to be so early in the morning. Then Sophie's voice saying she might be more excited about Joanne meeting George than George meeting Sunny provided a friendly boost of confidence. And courage. "Just getting their humans out to talk to new humans can make a huge difference for a lot of folks."

George laughed and brushed his shiny black curls back from his forehead.

"In that case, Sunny has her work cut out for her. At least Sophie would say so, and I can't disagree. I meet people all the time at work, and I know the parents around here with kids the same age as mine very well. Probably better than I should. But getting out and meeting someone who doesn't have either a tree emergency or a bunch of school-related drama will be a change of pace for sure. A good one."

He didn't stop rubbing Sunny's chin, but he looked up into Joanne's eyes. Something about his expression, or maybe a shift in the air in the cozy exam room, seemed to turn up the heat inside and out.

Sunny chose that instant to turn and carefully sniff Joanne from her chin to the top of her forehead, then give her a delicate kiss on the nose.

Surely a sign of approval, especially coming from a dog who'd endured what was probably her first tip-to-tail examination so graciously.

"I think a change of pace can be good, too," she said, hoping she didn't look too shy or goofy herself. "So, are we giving this girl her first series of shots today? I'll get my tech to send these samples out to make sure, but I'm not expecting to find any trouble. I'd say she's about as healthy as she is sweet."

"If she's even half that healthy, we won't have any trouble for a long time to come. I want to give her everything she needs to get started off right in her new life. I have to say she had pretty good timing, showing up right when I was contemplating what to do next, with my newly empty nest and all."

No matter how hard Joanne's sometimes paranoid side tried, she couldn't find a trace of anything needy or overly mopey in George's words or his eyes. Just like his sister had all but suggested, he really did seem ready for the adjustments in his life.

Being willing to take on a stray—even one as lovely as Sunny—spoke well of his character no matter who was doing the talking.

"One thing I always tell new animal guardians is bringing a pet into your life can change everything. And that kind of change can do us all so much good. I'll go grab her shots, and we'll get you on your way."

3

GEORGE WATCHED Joanne give Sunny a return kiss on the nose before she walked out of the exam room and closed the door.

Before he could gather the giddy whirl of his thoughts into some kind of order, his until-then quiet and calm dog let out a bunch of short, yippy barks, wagging her tail furiously. She stared at the door, as if willing the woman she'd just met to pleaseplease*please* come back.

Kind of the way George felt, but Sunny was a lot more demonstrative and honest about it.

His phone buzzed in his pocket, and he wondered whether that was one of his kids, impatient to hear more about their new sibling, or his sister, who would no doubt be a lot more curious about George's new acquaintance.

Before she'd fallen head over heels in love with

a wonderful guy they'd met during one of those tree emergencies, Sophie had been slipping over to the cynical side when it came to love. She'd been a hundred-percent onboard with George's decision to focus on his kids first for a long time, only shifting to Team Romance when her niece and nephew started mentioning it over the summer.

Now between those kids taking their first bittersweet steps out into the world and her own newly lovestruck ways, he had the feeling Sophie would give him a solid kick on the backside if he didn't take a chance.

Or at least let Joanne know he was interested.

So he wasn't entirely surprised to find a text message from Sophie waiting for him.

All good with your new girl? I mean your dog, of course. But I am curious what you think about our wonderful Dr. Robinette, too.

She'd added a silly emoji face that looked curious, with a question mark floating above its head for good measure.

Not because she had any suspicion George would miss her point, of course. But only because she was about as wicked and evil and rotten as any kid sister could possibly be.

Sunny carefully stepped down from the examination table, took a few steps to sniff loudly at the door handle, then sat in front of George and stared intently into his eyes.

Her addition was a brisk sneeze that he was sure carried more than a trace of impatience about Joanne not coming back into the room yet.

No more subtle than Sophie, as it turned out, even if Sunny wasn't even trying to hide her feelings.

"I take it you approve of Dr. Robinette? Even after getting your temperature taken?"

He had no choice but to interpret her low *woof* and increased tail-and-backside-wagging velocity as agreement.

George tapped out a quick reply to Sophie, trying to head off the inevitable phone call if he didn't answer fast enough. A habit he'd started between them, and regretted more often than not.

My new girl is doing great, thank you for checking on her. Nice and healthy, just waiting for a couple of shots. We're both enjoying Dr. Robinette's company, since you asked.

"So what should I do here, Sunny? Wait and see what happens?"

Sunny let out one of the long, dramatic sighs George was already falling in love with, this one energetic enough that her lips flapped a little.

"Or maybe I should see if she wants to go for a walk with us? How about that?"

Now Sunny repeated her earlier play bow, stretching out her front feet and lowering her chest almost to the floor. Her tail waved in the air, and her triangle ears perked toward the door, the black one standing at attention.

George wasn't quite sure he was ready to follow all of Sunny's suggestions or advice, even though he'd always heard a dog was the best judge of human character. Ivy Gweddon—one of his favorite people in town and companion to a long line of incredibly sweet redbone hounds— swore she'd never gone wrong when she let a smart dog tell her whether a person was good or bad.

Of course Sunny had also loved Mr. Seagon on sight, as any sensible living creature would just about have to.

"I think I'll take your advice then, silly girl. Assuming I don't lose my nerve first."

The door handle turned, and Sunny scooted herself backward and sat on George's feet, for all the world like she didn't want Joanne to know she'd been staring at the door.

Between that and Joanne's smile when she walked back in, George suspected he giggled more than he meant to.

"Everything okay in here?" Joanne said, putting three syringes down on the counter. "Sounds like you two are having a good time."

"You could say that. I think Sunny was hoping you were coming back."

Johanne shook her head, and her blush sent

those delicious quivers wandering all over George's body again.

"Well, she might change her mind once she realizes she's getting shots. I know the book Mr. Seagon gave you will give you plenty of information, but do you have any questions for me?"

Sunny pushed herself hard against George's legs, and he felt her tail thumping back and forth between his heels. She pointed her nose straight up in the air and managed to stare right into his eyes.

If he couldn't be encouraged by this amazing girl, who'd appeared out of the woods just that morning and decided to trust him to be a nice human, George knew he might as well take himself back home and sit in the corner.

And he had no desire to do that now, no matter how melancholy he'd felt just a couple of hours ago sitting on the porch of his empty house.

"I have about a hundred questions," he said, rubbing under Sunny's chin for courage. "And I'm sure I'll have a lot more after that. But just one right now. Want to go for a walk with me and Sunny sometime? Maybe give us a few pointers on picking out a new leash and collar before we go?"

Joanne's red lips parted in a smile, and George's heart did somersaults right there in his chest.

"I'd be delighted to, George. I believe I've got a leash and collar in the back that will fit her just right until you can get her a new one. How about this evening after work? I'd bet Kay's Café would be happy to pack a picnic dinner for all three of us."

Sunny answered before he could, stepping forward and pushing her nose into Joanne's hand. George hoped he'd get the chance to hold her hand himself before too many days passed.

"I'd never argue with such a good judge of character, or such great company for dinner."

KARI KILGORE

AUTHOR OF PUNGENT JUSTICE AND WHAT BREAKS A MAN

THE SIREN'S YOWL

To my sweet Lorelei

*Thank you for bringing yourself out of the cold
and into my life*

THE SIREN'S YOWL

I HAD no idea how much taking in a cat was going to change my life.

Mainly because that impulse decision likely ended up *saving* my life.

Well, I can't really claim credit for something as clear as a decision, and I doubt it was any kind of human-variety impulse that brought us together.

The truth is my first sweet cat sort of brought herself in, squeezing through an open living room window that I *still* swear wasn't wide enough for her to fit through. One of those old, overly painted double-hung models that would manage to work itself open a few inches if you didn't basically slam it shut and latch it tight. Whenever the evening sunlight hit it, or the wind blew in the right direction, or sometimes because the day ended in the letter Y.

Just another quirk of living on the second floor of an antique, absurdly expensive building in a great location that I never thought much about before a cat decided to claim me as her own.

But when I dragged myself upstairs that evening, about to fall over exhausted from working too long for what turned out to be no good reason, a pretty little calico girl was waiting for me on my kitchen table.

Staring at me with big green eyes, stub tail wrapped as far around her feet as it would go. Fitting perfectly between my pink seashell napkin holder and salt and pepper shakers that look like the classic brown and black law reference books that weren't available online back in those days.

She hadn't knocked a single thing over that I could find, or even gotten into the trash after the empty tuna can I'd tossed after I glopped the contents onto a sandwich I'd have for lunch at my desk, as usual.

Funny thing is I didn't jump or yell or anything. Sounds strange to say it, but I don't recall being startled or even surprised.

I just opened the door, flipped on the light, saw her, and shrugged.

It had been that kind of week, I guess.

She was kind of dirty that night, all the white on her feet and belly a little dingy. A condition she would never again allow herself to get into as long as she lived. Probably from living outside, or maybe from however she climbed up onto my downstairs neighbor's roof and pushed herself through the tiny gap in the window.

And she didn't seem any more surprised than I did. We both kind of sized each other up, blinked, and got on with it.

I named her Lorelei for what might sound like an especially nerdy reason, but it made perfect sense, then and now. I wish I could say I named her after the mythological siren, with the way things turned out. I can't claim anything nearly that clever.

I was in kind of a Styx phase, listening to a lot of their music in the car. That was the music that cheered me up when I needed it, and I needed it a lot right then.

The cassette player I had was pretty fancy for 1989, and CDs and players were still way too expensive for my blood. Of course iPods and streaming music weren't even daydreams back then. So we had to plan out what we wanted to listen to and pack it along with us.

Hard to believe, I know.

That Styx song *Lorelei* has always been one of my favorites, and it was playing when I parked. Simple as that.

I didn't have any kind of cat food, but I did have

another can of tuna. That and some water got her settled in right away.

Tired as I was, I knew she'd need the toilet before I would likely have a chance to get to the store with another early morning breathing down my workaholic neck.

Not much choice but to properly close that window, get back in the car—with *Lorelei* the song starting in the middle and making me smile—and haul myself out to the all-night grocery for litter and a litterbox. I grabbed a bunch of canned food because she liked the tuna so much, too.

And simple as that, I had my first-ever cat.

I wasn't Lorelei's first human. I know because when I took her to the vet a few days later to get her checked out, turned out she'd already been spayed. Once the vet showed me where the scar was, I felt it plain as day.

I did try to find her people, even though I wanted her to stay as soon as I saw her perched calm and comfortable on my kitchen table. Asked around at the vet's office, grocery store, post office. Even put an ad in the local paper, which I by then desperately hoped no one would answer.

No one ever did.

Lorelei was too laid back and well-mannered to have come from any kind of bad situation, but I still wonder how she got away.

I'm not *quite* willing to believe it was because

she knew how much I needed her, unless I'm feeling especially nostalgic. Or grateful.

Once we both knew she was there to stay, I wondered how I'd managed to live alone for so long.

I'd moved to that cozy second-floor apartment with my boyfriend a few years before, both of us brimming with excitement about starting our lives in that small, friendly Midwestern city.

Me working at an up-and-coming law firm not too many blocks away—walkable when I had time and energy and the weather was good—certain I would be on the path to partner before long. Spending money I didn't yet have on my Serious Young Attorney wardrobe of black and charcoal gray pantsuits, and expensive but comfortable shoes.

Him teaching history at a college on the other side of town, with his eye on tenure and writing a pile of books, spending a lot less on a selection of coordinating slacks, sport jackets, and proper Earnest Young Professor loafers.

Bright future right on target, happiness ahead for everyone, right?

Just over a year later, my boyfriend decided he needed a different future in a bigger city.

With a different girlfriend.

Who'd been one of his students the previous semester.

I figured then and now it said a hell of a lot about our time as good friends before we became short-lived lovers that we managed to stay in touch after that gruesome episode.

It took a couple more years before I realized my future at the firm was pretty damn overcast, too. Rather than cruising along the fast track to partner, I'd veered into the painfully slow, work-yourself-to-death-and-never-see-any-reward lane.

Several of the new associates who started when I did were traveling on that same dead-end, no-exit-lane together, as it turned out. Rot and trouble had set in before we ever got there, bad enough that the whole thing would collapse before anyone who stayed knew what hit them.

Well, I suppose the ones who not only didn't stop the rot but invited it in and asked it to make itself at home knew.

But that's a little bit ahead of what happened with me and Lorelei, even though it *is* part of the same story.

The autumn Lorelei moved in, I'd been whittling down a backlog of what I thought were small-time criminal cases in my non-existent spare time.

Pro-bono work mostly. Stepping in to help folks who couldn't afford to pay and were getting lost in an overloaded public defender's or district attorney's backlist. Putting in an unreasonable number of hours even for a young associate, with delusions of impressing the partners.

I wish I could say I truly wanted to do some good in the world instead. Helping misguided people who needed a second chance get their lives turned around, or helping victims of those crimes get justice and move on with *their* lives.

Sounds great to me now, and I actually do more of that kind of work with every passing year and encourage eager, energetic young associates to do the same. Along with a lecture about doing it more carefully than I used to.

Back then?

I'm not proud to admit I was after numbers and billable hours. Trying to pull myself ahead in a ridiculously talented field instead of feeling like everything else was moving so fast I had to sprint to stand still. Working myself to death so I wouldn't slip down to last place.

The partners had no idea of what I or any other associate was up to, of course. They were too busy trying to keep their own asses out of the quicksand.

Not that any of us fresh-out-of-school hotshots had any clue.

I *am* proud to admit having that cat choose *my* window to squeeze herself through kept me sane during the long, cold months of that winter. She gave me a reason to come home, to actually take the occasional day off.

Lorelei loved to snuggle up on the couch with me, in my lap or warm across my shoulders, while I worked or watched TV or read a book or did nothing but stare out at the snow falling.

She slept with me too, curled against my back or chest or tucked into the curve of my knees.

Her good-morning chirps helped me get moving whether I was dragging myself into the office or tackling as much as research and writing as I could manage at home.

I hadn't grown up with pets besides my mother's elaborate fish tank, so I had no idea how much an animal could add to my life. I'm sure my mother would say the fish did the same for her, but I doubt she could convince me.

What fish ever purred someone to sleep after a rotten day? Or ran to meet them when they came home, no matter how late? With their adorable stubby tail held high and chattering up a storm like they couldn't wait to hear about your day and tell you everything that happened while you were gone?

No fish I've ever met or heard of.

It was Lorelei's habit of greeting me at the door and having so much to say that warned me.

That and the window.

I was every bit as tired as the night she first showed up, just about staggering up those outside steps with the wind and snow blowing me sideways against the brick building. Lugging my briefcase and one of those boxy leather litigation cases I'd been hauling around since my days on the high school debate team.

And an appropriately high-end purse, too, can't forget that. No one could get away with a simple backpack then, not to mention the sheer lunacy of putting the contents of said purse *inside* the brief-case like men did. At least in our image-conscious firm in that friendly Midwestern city, female associates had a far stricter dress code than the suit-and-tie-and-no-worries-about-makeup crowd.

Now I know we were just lucky this was in the pre-laptop-bag days.

The bigger problem was my mind was entirely on the juicy embezzlement case I was nose-deep in the middle of pre-trial madness for, rather than one I'd handled weeks before as part of my "minor crime" crusade. Not that anyone sane would have been thinking that way, even without my self-inflicted obscene workload.

This is an open-and-shut case of condemning myself through hindsight.

And yes, I do know how pointless that is. I'd tell a friend or colleague to stop beating themselves up over it in a heartbeat.

I suppose telling this story in the first place is my way of trying to give myself the same grace.

That night, I stumbled into the kitchen, dropped everything on the floor and shoved the door shut behind me, which was a trick in itself with the wind howling at my back in a cruel attempt to shove it right back open.

I hadn't even taken my usual just-got-home deep breath when I noticed something was wrong.

Not only was Lorelei not waiting for me—perched in her original spot on the kitchen table more often than not—or running down the hall with her half-length tail held high, burbling out her Happy Kitty Hour welcome no matter what time I dragged myself in.

She was somewhere in the apartment yowling.

Not in that awful, heartbreaking, help-me-I'm-really-hurt way that I can't stand to hear from any creature, human or otherwise.

This was her aggrieved "Get in here and fix this, underling!" yowl. Usually associated with an empty food dish, a toy knocked under the couch, or a door or drawer she'd decided simply should *not* be closed.

Instead of rushing to do her bidding, which would not likely have ended well, I closed my eyes and let out a gusty, poor-me sigh. Standing there with my back against the winter-cold steel door, stomach growling, stink of exhaust from cars and furnaces all over the city still in my nose.

I kicked off my shoes first, because even my sensible and costly low-heeled pumps were intolerable by the end of a sixteen-hour day.

The draft whispering across my toes added to Lorelei's ongoing complaints to finally get my attention.

Even with all the creaky older-building problems that apartment had—slow plumbing, not enough electrical outlets, floors so uneven a baseball would roll away from one wall all the way across to the other—it was heaven on bitterly cold winter nights.

The family who lived downstairs kept their heat cranked so high my power bills actually went *down* when the snow started flying. I'm quite certain I would have hated that little feature when my internally overheated passage into menopause really got rolling.

But back then, Lorelei and I both loved it.

The constantly warm floors were the best feature. No need to turn up the thermostat or pay for radiant-floor heating. That World War I Era charmer had it built right in.

So a draft cold enough to feel was more than enough to put me on alert, even if Lorelei hadn't been singing out the highly exasperated siren song of her people.

Another hard-to-imagine aspect of those days was how few people owned cellular phones. I wasn't earning nearly enough as a chronically overworked associate to shell out a few thousand dollars for one, much less keep up with the horrifying cost per minute.

But I *had* upgraded my endlessly tangle-corded landline phone for a cordless model a few years back. Around the time my ex decamped, along with his stubborn determination to never pay extra for modern technology when the old tech still more or less functioned.

Having the phone's base in the kitchen but enough range to wander all over the apartment delighted me to no end years before I carried a computer in my pocket.

I sang out a greeting to my agitated cat, apologizing for getting home so late. Promising her a quick and tasty dinner as soon as I called my senior partner and changed clothes.

Yes, even a cat who'd never set foot in a law office would have known a lowly associate wouldn't be calling *any* of the partners at that hour, but Lorelei wasn't the one I was trying to distract.

I grabbed the phone and hit one of the speed-dials on the base, trying not to giggle at who I'd decided to call for help. Then doing my best not to cry with relief when he picked up on the other end.

One of the silly and sort of macabre games my ex and I had played back in our dating, pre-living-together days might be called Worst Case Scenario. We'd have a few beers or a couple of cocktails, and think up the most horrible situations and figure out how to game our way out of them.

Truly *awful* things like being kidnapped, getting paralyzed except for our eyes, or getting caught in a war zone on an overseas trip.

I know how it sounds to someone living an ordinary life, or someone who's actually been in a terrible situation. All I can say in our defense is I was studying criminal law when we met, and he was studying the history of warfare.

The fact that such black humor drew us together —combined with researching and inventing the most bizarre incidents we could to impress each other—should have let us know our relationship was doomed.

Or that we were a perfect match after all, and life just took us in other directions.

That night, with a warning draft across my toes and my heart pounding out of my chest, I put one of our make-believe strategies into all-too-real practice.

As soon as he answered, I started telling him about my day, which I hadn't done since he shouted his way out the door with a garbage bag full of his Earnest Young Professor wardrobe slung over his shoulder.

But I did it using prime numbers. I described the most mundane tasks you could imagine, but in counts of two, three, and five, then seven, eleven, and thirteen.

Two flat tires on the way in, three emergency notes at my desk, five cups of coffee before noon, followed by seven billable hours working on eleven cases before I had a late, long meeting with thirteen presenters.

All a bunch of nonsense, obviously. All while I stepped right back into those same uncomfortable shoes and opened the refrigerator door.

And bless his heart and shower him with tenure and great sex and huge book deals until the day he dies, he remembered. He caught on right away.

He told me he had seventeen office hours scheduled that week, with nineteen different disgruntled students, and a faculty meeting with twenty-three bullet points. Then he asked me to let him know when I'd like to get together with twenty-nine of our old college friends for a reunion.

A couple of tears might have made it down my cheeks when I told him I'd let him know on the thirty-first.

Then I hung up, and deployed the foolproof cat-retrieval device I'd gotten out of the fridge.

I opened the plastic wrapper on a piece of plain old American cheese.

Just like my ex, Lorelei did exactly what I needed her to.

She streaked down the hall and into the kitchen,

yowling all the way. I gave her a corner of the cheese and tucked her inside my coat and under my arm. I shoved the rest into my mouth as I backed us right out that door and into the gale-force wind, with my unwieldy purse and nothing else slung over my shoulder.

I stopped in at my downstairs neighbors' to tell them to either get everyone out now, or stay inside and make sure their windows and doors were shut, *and* locked tight.

And I got myself and my cat safely into the car.

But we didn't go more than a few hundred feet.

I'm not sure if this makes me a risk-taker or brave or just someone who was fixated on vengeance. Either way, I parked down the block where I could see both the living room window and my kitchen door. The car's heater was still charged up from my drive home, so my toes weren't even cold.

I wanted to make sure whoever was inside didn't get away, of course.

But what I really wanted was to watch the police—who showed up with truly eerie speed that night if no other time in my life—take down the asshole who'd broken into my apartment.

So Lorelei and I got to enjoy the sight of two officers march a screaming, thrashing, furious woman out the door and down the stairs. Once they had her in their squad car and hit the lights, I flagged down the second car to let them know I was okay.

And to let them know I needed a few minutes to get my *extremely* good cat back upstairs and feed her before I joined them at the station to do what needed to be done.

I had to cover up the broken window, too.

The one I knew about before the police mentioned it to me.

Because I'd recognized that draft over my toes from the days before a cat let herself in through my self-opening window. I'd gotten into an unshakable habit of keeping that and all the windows latched after the first time I came home to my sweet Lorelei sitting on the kitchen table.

The same Lorelei who somehow knew to warn me with her siren song before I strolled unknowing into a length of rope, a knife, duct tape, and a woman hell-bent on using them.

Turned out she wasn't too happy with the guilty verdict I'd helped get against her baby sister over that summer: part of my futile impress-the-partners-by-taking-on-pro-bono-cases campaign.

Never mind that baby sister had a habit of breaking and entering the homes of elderly folks who lived alone, hoping to score drugs or jewelry or whatever she could sell.

One older gentleman and I finally got the charges to stick.

Big sister decided to deliver her own form of justice in return for what I'd done in putting baby sister away.

They didn't end up with adjoining jail cells or anything that cutesy, or even matching sentences. As a matter of fact, big sister ended up doing more time.

I'm honestly sad to say that kind of activity turned out to be a lifelong habit for both of them. But as far as I know, they never turned to potential kidnapping again.

On the other hand, in all the many years that have gone by since then, I've had more than my share of good fortune.

I ended up moving south to a much bigger city before my first firm imploded and took too many of my fellow associates down with it. I made partner at last after busting my ass and earning it, partly because I wasn't spinning my wheels trying to impress people who were neck-deep in their own disaster.

Ended up in a happier marriage than I could have imagined the night of the break-in, too. With a better match than I could have possibly had with my successful professor ex, who I'm friends with to this day.

All with a healthy respect for locked windows and doors, security systems, and a deep appreciation for the comfort of a phone and GPS in my pocket.

And I've had more than my fair share of wonderful cats and a few dogs along the way. I couldn't imagine a home without them, no matter how much time I spend with a lint-roller or mini-vacuum extracting their hair from my power suits.

But none of them ever quite matched up to my amazing Lorelei, who used her disagreeable siren's yowl to warn me away from danger rather than tempt me into it.

KARI KILGORE

AUTHOR OF FANTASTIC SIDE TRIPS AND THE DREAM THIEF

The Storms That Save You

A MISFORTUNE AND MAGIC STORY

For everyone who lends a helping hand

THE STORMS THAT SAVE YOU

DESPITE ONLY LASTING for a few short weeks, Genlifeh was the most important time in the great desert city of Profant.

Without the torrential rain and fierce storms and winds, life wouldn't be pleasant or likely even possible the rest of the year. People, animals, and plants alike enjoyed their time to rest, to take in as much moisture as they possibly could against the return of burning sun and scouring, parched breezes.

Partly because no one else was out and about—and partly because his parents forbade him—Hildar Bacalan loved nothing more than wandering the hidden parts of the city while life-giving water poured from the sky.

Investigating his home without crowds.

Observing how ordinary spaces transformed with the addition of so much sudden moisture.

The orderly lines of streets and buildings and the city wall never changed, not as much as he would have liked.

The gravel that lined the streets in their precise and well-maintained angles turned from brown and dull to black and glistening. Losing their thick coating of dust from countless feet, wagon wheels, and landhorses passing through day after day, month after month, for most of the arid year.

All the noise of hooves and voices, clanking and creaking wagons, shouting and laughter fell away under the steady roar of Genlifeh wind and rain, startling blasts of thunder, and blinding flashes of lightning.

The desert's own cinnamon aroma faded, along with the usual daily background of baking bread and roasting meat, and the variety of pleasant landhorse scents. Hildar only smelled the wonderful rain: fresh and mineral, the air sometimes electric with ozone.

These days of the Genlifeh monsoon were the only time an endless stream of travelers wasn't entering and exiting the city, sustaining the power of the city and the barony itself. The majority of those passing through knew to time their arrival around the downpours, when the roads into and out of the city were reliably overwhelmed.

Lack of good drainage turned them into impass-able bogs full of mud and untrustworthy footing, and no chance of assistance or rescue once the storms settled in.

But a handful always seemed to arrive either too late to leave or after suffering through the last few miles of awful travel. Sometimes due to delay along the way, occasionally because of poor planning. No one in Profant had ever figured out whether these unwilling guests would be grateful for the most basic of shelter or angry at having their journey interrupted.

Hildar had to admit the lack of entertainment, places to eat, or merchants to buy from or sell to likely made for a less interesting stay than the unwary could have imagined.

No other easy path existed across the huge continent of Hanferthen from the high mountains of Fadlonah in the east to rugged coastal Maestar, the city of airhorses far to the west. From bustling Casai along the warm southern Wrynath Sea, to the mysterious plateau of Dirgelan many days to the north, full of Honored Mages and their terrifying command of magic.

Without one of the rare and magnificent airhorses, or a sturdy boat and the skills to navigate the unpredictable seas, everyone must pass through Profant, no matter how weak or mighty.

That responsibility and power—and the danger

that came with it—weighed heavily on Hildar's mind even though he only had fourteen years. The decision of whether to take on that challenge loomed in his future and rarely left his thoughts.

Except during the excitement and focus of his wanderings in the rain.

Unlike the gravels going from brown to black, the buildings and the massive red stone wall that enclosed all of Profant simply turned darker red. Closer to the burgundy of Hildar's favorite spicy grain than their usual bloody hue.

He still loved standing in exactly the right spot, pressed against the wall's towering bulk, letting the shocking chill of the rain wash over his body and clear his mind as it sheeted down.

He'd learned early on to wear only his thinnest and lightest of tunics for his Genlifeh adventures, and breeches too short for a boy his age. He shouldn't have been seen outside his parents' huge residence with his knees showing, but he wanted everything to dry in his room before anyone noticed.

Baron Arvage and Baroness Tametha would have deeply disapproved of his private explorations for his choice of clothing alone.

The best places for Hildar's secretive and risky showers were where the wall had been purposely built with thrilling, subtle angles hundreds of years ago.

In dozens of locations he was sure most citizens of Profant never even noticed, the several-feet-thick stones of the wall stood slightly lower than the rest. The slope was too gradual to see in normal weather, creating a series of tiny peaks and valleys all along the vast stretch of the city's protection.

The entire wall tilted in toward those low spots, as well as inward toward the city.

The slight modifications were enough to produce heavy columns of water collected from the red stone that poured into the city's vital underground cistern, even larger than the great stretch of buildings and streets enclosed by the wall.

The streets themselves avoided flooding and puddles with careful layers of porous rock and sand that let water trickle through and into the same crucial supply.

In order to enjoy his exhilarating time under water flowing fast and hard enough to knock him down if he wasn't careful, Hildar balanced his bare feet on a grid of chilly metal bars set into stone channels in the ground.

His feet couldn't *quite* fit between the gaps in the slick bars if he held them flat and placed them carefully. And even if one did, the muscles of his calves or thighs would certainly keep him from slipping further.

But possibly not until he managed to twist his knee, or tear tendons, or break bones.

The simple indignity of getting stuck—with the possible risk of falling at the wrong angle and fighting gallons of high-speed water intent on drowning him for his trespass—would be more than bad enough even if he didn't manage to hurt himself.

Nowhere near bad enough to keep Hildar where he was supposed to be on the first stormy morning of Genlifeh.

Another of his favorite haunts while a year's-worth of rain washed away dust and set the city's carefully tended crops to an outburst of growth was the cistern itself.

Closely supervised visits with teachers and other children his age years ago had awakened his fascination with the constructed lake underneath the city, and he'd returned a few more times with his father as part of his later training.

But those brief, supervised strolls through thousands of rough, red columns carved into the very bedrock under the city never quite satisfied Hildar. Partly because the water was calm and serene on those days. So much so that it reflected their hand-held torches—both conjured and natural fire—exactly like a flawless mirror. Already settled months before monsoon, and usually partly drained with Profant's constant need for it.

The rain of those precious few weeks was drawn

upward for drinking and bathing, cooking and cleaning, for the rest of the long, dry year.

Important as it was, *using* the water wasn't nearly as exciting as how it was collected.

So on the days he could escape parents, siblings, teachers, and friends during Genlifeh—and when he'd had his daily fill of enjoying the high-pressure torrent cascading over his flesh—Hildar nearly ran along the maze-like red-stone corridors of the baron's residence.

Wearing a dry tunic and breeches along with proper sandals, but his skin still chilly and tingling from the deluge. Thick brown hair damp and curling, gray eyes and keen ears alert for signs of anyone else nearby. Only a few dim torches lit the way, casting a warm, magical bluish light rather than the smoky yellow of natural fire.

Following the rock-solid sense of direction he seemed to have been born with, he unerringly knew which turn to take even in the faint light, which stair to descend. While the roar of the storm over his head grew fainter and the joy of his solo defiance grew stronger.

He'd passed well into the lower levels now, where the city's food, weapons, and precious herbs and medicines were stored above the main entrance to the cistern. Everything kept far enough from levels of humidity incredible to desert dwellers to prevent spoiling, and supposedly protected from curious folks wandering inside simply by being underneath the baron's guarded residence.

In other words, safe from those who didn't live there, or weren't sufficiently determined to explore anyway.

In all the years of his furtive Genlifeh explorations, Hildar had rarely met anyone else out and about, either in the forbidden areas of the baron's residence or out in the streets. Most residents of Profant who weren't tending to the unexpectedly stranded travelers took their chance to rest and enjoy the rain. Catching up on sleep or reading or beloved pastimes, refilling their minds and bodies as the cistern below their feet did the same.

Even animals from huge landhorses to fowl and goats all the way to the maddeningly clever vermin and the fascinating *slemich* that hunted them generally slipped into a state of near-hibernation during Genlifeh.

But on this day, Hildar tried to skid a halt when one of the knee-high, furry slemich darted out in front of him and let out a dismaying screech. He ended up leaping over it instead.

After a few staggering steps to regain his balance, he turned to watch it, hands on his knees as he tried to catch his breath.

The slemich crouched on the stone floor, glaring at him with huge, glowing violet eyes, whipping its long, narrow tail back and forth. This one had short, gleaming fur the same color as the sparkling tan sands of the desert around Profant. Hildar had seen others that matched the red stone or brown gravel, and heard that slemich in other lands blended in with their surroundings as well.

Green near forests or grasslands, white near snow. Vibrant shades of the local sand along the Wrynath Sea, black or gray in the rough mountains. He'd heard the ones around Maestar were much larger, though still nowhere as big as the huge wild-cats that were the bane of keepers of fowl, sheep, and bovines alike.

All of the slemich were expert hunters of what-ever was close to hand, and most of them happily friendly and affectionate when given the chance.

"Were you *trying* to trip me?"

Hildar smiled when the slemich raised itself to its full height, all four muscular legs straight. Its thin, translucent wings were still folded at its sides, and he could barely see the membranes that attached the wings to the creature's thighs.

Slemich weren't great flyers the way airhorses were, but once they climbed to their hunting perches, they were incredible gliders.

"Here, I won't hurt you."

He knelt and held out one hand, wishing he had some sort of food to share. A few of his friends had slemich that lived openly inside their rooms or houses, brave and secure enough to snuggle in whatever lap was available when they weren't busy protecting food stores.

He wasn't sure whether his parents would permit such familiarity in his own rooms, but Hildar took every chance he could to stroke a slemich's silky fur.

The slemich took a few quick, graceful steps forward, close enough to a torch for him to see the rounded tips of its huge triangular ears and the constantly moving black nose. Two lighter crests of raised golden hair started at those ears and ran down its long, muscular neck before joining into a stripe that went all the way to the tip of its tail.

Slemich had softer features than the drawings of wildcats he'd seen, but their stubby claws were every bit as sharp when they ran them out.

Hildar shifted his weight, and the scraping noise of his sandal sent the slemich down into a crouch again. But it didn't run away.

"Maybe I can bring food next time I pass this way. See if you want to be friends."

He stood and the slemich did the same, blinking those beautiful violet eyes.

Smiling, Hildar backed up a few steps. The slemich followed, still low to the ground.

"Okay, I won't look at you then."

He turned and kept going, strolling rather than his earlier dash. Every time he glanced back, the slemich was keeping itself about five paces behind.

"I wonder if you'll follow me all the way back to my rooms? Or down to the cistern? I heard they used to stock fish down there a long time ago. I'm sure you would have loved that."

But when he walked past one of the storeroom stairwells off to the right, the slemich screeched again, not quite as loudly as when he'd nearly tripped over it. The sound was an eerie, somehow mournful rise and fall, not that different from the great hunting birds that sometimes circled over the sewage fields outside the city, but much softer.

When Hildar turned, it sat right beside the doorway, mouth open and already huge eyes wide. A row of tidy teeth and impressive fangs gleamed with a fainter glow the same shade as its eyes.

"Sorry, you have somewhere you need to be?"

He took another step backward, and it stood with its wings raised, the furred skin stretched so thin he could see torchlight through it.

Frowning, Hildar stepped forward. Once, twice.

Now the slemich lowered its wings let out the same warbling hum he'd heard when they were content, eating or curled up in someone's lap.

As soon as he stepped away again, the comforting sound stopped. One more step brought a short screech and a shivery flap of its wings.

The slemich stared at him, and Hildar realized the poor thing's whole body was shivering. He stepped forward again, bending his knees so maybe he wouldn't be so tall and threatening.

Instead of relaxing or warbling again, the slemich turned and took two steps down the stairwell. It stopped and looked back up at Hildar, now shaking its wings as if trying to get rid of the rain so far above their heads that the roar was gone.

"I don't even know what's down there, but it's pretty clear you want me to find out. No chance of me going to get help, huh? Not that I especially want to explain what I'm doing here in the first place."

Hildar only waited long enough to retrieve the torch, lifting the short ceramic container barely longer than his hand from the wall. The seldom-used passages and stairs under the baron's residence were generally unlit.

The blue conjured light floated a tiny bit above the curved surface as it shifted itself to remain centered. He didn't have the magic himself to make it brighter or longer-lived, but he knew enough to take care not to drop it and leave himself in darkness.

When he looked down at the slemich again—now fluttering its wings and stamping its front feet in a clear show of impatience—he hoped he'd found something far more interesting than exploring forbidden areas.

The slemich gave a higher pitched warbling trill

when Hildar stepped down behind it, then it scurried ahead much faster than he could. The stairwell curved enough that he soon lost sight of the creature, and its near-silent feet were no help. It stopped several times to wait for him, holding one foot curled near its broad chest, before continuing on.

They passed two closed doors set into the rough walls before the slemich stopped, sitting in the middle of another corridor. This one only had torches far enough apart to show which direction to walk rather than to actually light the passage.

"Okay, I'm here now. What did you want me to see? Found too many vermin in the stores to handle by yourself? Or maybe a thief?"

Chills raced over Hildar's flesh at his own words, and an idea he hadn't even considered. Some herders and farmers trained slemich to do more than hunt, though they never seemed to lose that skill. Had someone taught this one to raise the alert over an intruder?

One he might not want to meet on his own, with nothing more than a torch to protect himself with?

For a second, he thought the scrabbling noise was the slemich trying to get his attention, even it hadn't made a move to go left or right.

In fact, it wasn't even looking at him. It stared intently and unblinking at the dark space where the last curve of the stairs met the floor.

That's where the scrabbling came from.

Had the slemich found something too large to handle on its own?

Possibly too large for *him* to handle, too?

"If you're not willing to face whatever's under there," Hildar whispered, "with your teeth and claws and huge eyes, I probably should go get help."

A hissing noise from the darkness startled him nearly enough to drop the conjured torch after all. But he caught himself right before he bolted up the stairs.

Because that hissing didn't sound like any sort of animal, dangerous or not.

It sounded like another person, frightened and whispering just like he was. He doubted a thief would be hiding like this, cowering so close to the storerooms, with nothing but a slemich and a boy keeping them from simply leaving.

"Is someone there?" Hildar said, raising his voice but making sure not to shout. "I'm not going to hurt you."

Hildar counted his breath until he got to ten, mainly because that was easier to control than his racing heart.

"I've got a light, so I'm going to look under the stairs. I might be able to help you."

He looked at the slemich, still watching the darkness without cowering or trembling at all. It only sat with its long tail straight out behind and its wings tucked close against its ribs.

One of the other rumors he'd heard about slemich was they had a strong habit of disliking people who meant them harm: a habit perhaps driven by their own magic. And the ones who lived with people took that further and included anyone who meant their companions harm.

Unless he was willing to walk away, Hildar was going to have to trust that rumor of their good judgement.

He moved forward, holding the light as far out in front as he could, wishing he could do the simplest magic of lightening the color or focusing it to shine in one direction instead of all around.

The slemich stayed where it was, and stayed calm.

When he was close enough to touch the side of the stairs, and the space left in front of him barely came up to his waist, he spotted the toe of a pale green leather shoe, with a rounded design he'd never seen before. He was drawing breath to say something else when the shoe moved, and a rustling noise let him know the person was moving.

Hildar backed up, and gasped when a boy much taller than he stepped out into the hallway.

The boy wore much heavier woven breeches and tunic than Hildar's, both of them a dark brown that would be far too hot under Profant's typical blazing sun. Tall as he was, the boy was slender to the point of being bony, with thick blond hair and sickly pale skin.

His hands trembled when he held them up, and his voice was surprisingly deep even though he didn't look much older than Hildar's fourteen years.

The words sounded...*rounded* to Hildar's ear, with all the sharp edges worn off by the boy's slow, gentle way of speaking.

"I'm sorry. I didn't mean to bother anyone, truly."

Hildar blinked and smiled.

"You're not bothering me at all. I didn't mean to scare you. Why are you hiding down here?"

The boy squeezed his lips together and shook his head, staring down at his strange shoes.

"I'm not going to hurt you," Hildar said, wanting more than anything to make this boy feel better. "I couldn't get you into trouble even if I wanted to. I'm just another kid, and I'm not supposed to be down here either. I'm Hildar."

The boy looked up under his eyebrows, his face twitching into a smile that disappeared at once.

But he didn't seem quite so afraid now.

"I'm Dewin. I think I've heard your name from someone here. Is that your slemich?"

Hildar didn't forget Dewin hadn't said anything about why he was hiding under a staircase deep inside the baron's residence, but he pretended to.

He glanced down at the slemich, now watching the two of them and making its contented warbling sound again.

"This one isn't mine, but I'd love to have one that would stay in my rooms. Are you staying here? In this house, I mean, not just in Profant. That might be how you heard my name. Was that you, whispering? Is someone else down here?"

Dewin rubbed his arms and looked around, like he was expecting someone to jump out of the shadowy hallway.

"I didn't want the slemich to show anyone where I was. I know how that sounds, but that's what you heard."

"Can you... Why are you down here?"

"We weren't supposed to be here even one night. *They* weren't. But then the storm came, like no rain I've ever seen in my life. Not even in the farmlands where I lived that can't survive without it. Still they tried to keep going, broke a wagon wheel not far past your gate here for their trouble."

"I'm sorry, Dewin, I don't know who you mean. Your family?"

Dewin closed his eyes and shook his head.

"Not my family, no. They'd never... My family wasn't the kind to take people away when they don't want to go. They got sick, my family. I did too, but I got better. Something bad in the grain, maybe, made the bovines and fowl and everything else spoil. The traders that came through said they could make us all better. I'm the only one who still draws breath."

Hildar shivered harder than he ever did after standing in the pouring rain outside.

"Are those traders here? Did they bring you here?"

Dewin nodded. "I'm supposed to be in the stables with the landhorses. They treat the landhorses better than me and the others. Feed them better food, let them eat more. I guess because they paid coin for them. Taking us to Casai to labor at the docks there. I tried to hide. These traders, they look fine and wealthy, and they demanded to see the baron. That's why I'm here."

Hildar hoped the churning in his stomach didn't show on his face. If his parents or anyone else in Profant knew what had happened to Dewin, the people who'd brought him wouldn't be sheltering in the baron's residence or anywhere else.

Taking people against their will, for work or any other reason, wasn't tolerated here or in any other city he knew of in Hanferthen. Too many wars had been fought over that in the past to let it take root again.

He'd hoped the rumors of such things happening away from cities weren't true. But he'd heard all his life to do what he could to make sure people in such a dreadful trap never passed through

Profant's gates without doing what he could to help them.

"You did hear my name, Dewin, because I'm the baron's son." Hildar held up his own hands when Dewin jerked back. "No, I'm not going to do anything bad, at least I don't mean to. Do you want to get away from these traders? Are there others who want to get away?"

Dewin hesitated, then drew himself up as tall as he could.

"I didn't want to go with them in the first place, but I was too sick to stop them. This is the first time in all the days since they took me from my home that I've been strong enough to hide and try to get away. There are others who need your help too."

Hildar's heart thudded in his chest again, and his belly tumbled and rolled like all the rain pouring over the walls. This time because of excitement and hope rather than fear.

He reached out and gently touched Dewin's arm, trying not to wince at how pitifully thin it was.

"Will you wait here while I go get my parents? They know what to do, how to help you all *stay* away. None of you will be punished, I promise. The ones who took you against your wishes won't be so lucky."

Dewin half-smiled, and the mischief in it made it clear he hadn't always been so serious and scared.

"But *you* might get into trouble, from the way

you look right now. You said earlier you're not supposed to be down here yourself."

That surprised Hildar into a laugh, and both boys laughed when the slemich paused its warbling with its head tilted to one side, gigantic ears tilted forward nearly over its luminous violet eyes.

It rustled its wings and curled up on the floor with a long sigh, eyes closed, using its long tail as a slender pillow for its twitching black nose.

"I'm not supposed to be down here, no," Hildar said. "But maybe I won't get into so much trouble since this slemich helped me find you. I'm hoping my parents will let it stay with me if it wants to."

Dewin nodded, and the breath he let out sounded a lot like the slemich's resting sigh. He settled to the ground himself, leaning against the rough wall with his long legs stretched out rather than crouching in the darkness.

"That one would make a good companion, I'd say. She's smart enough to take good care of herself, so you know she's a good hunter, and she's friendly. That's the kind we always kept with us when...when I was younger."

"How do you know this one's female? I never can tell."

Dewin leaned forward and stroked the slemich's head, getting a soft warble in return.

"Partly because she *is* so smart. That and her golden crest. The males either have a darker one or don't have one at all. Just the kind of thing you know growing up in the farmlands, I guess. They have magic too. They have to, since so many of the vermin do. That's why slemich so much better at catching them than people are."

Hildar squatted long enough to rub her head, smiling when she raised up enough lick his hand with her raspy tongue before settling back down with a sweet hum. He'd only heard whisperings that slemich had magic, but after meeting this one, he believed it.

He might face a well-deserved scolding before the day was out, but he didn't care nearly so much about that as he would have that morning. The idea of possibly serving as baron himself someday wasn't quite as intimidating as it had been, either.

"I think we'll have a lot to learn from each other, Dewin. I'll tell you all about the Genlifeh storms that saved you, maybe over a good meal once you have a chance to catch your breath. I'm glad to be the one to welcome you to Profant."

KARI KILGORE

AUTHOR OF AT THE HEART OF IT ALL AND FANTASTIC SIDE TRIPS

The Part That Loves the Most

*For Cathy, my Mom, and everyone
who's helped bring animals into our lives*

THE PART THAT LOVES THE MOST

WHEN IT CAME to rebirth and renewal, no time or place on earth could possibly be better than spring-time in the Appalachian Mountains.

Right then Clara could see far too much evidence of that glorious reality to dispute, no matter how much her beat-up heart might want to.

Traces of frost lingered on the still-bare branches of the oak tree closest to her house, but in its shadow, she spotted vivid purple crocuses peeking through the brown carpet of last year's leaves. The much smaller redbuds on the hillside hadn't quite put on their own purple show, but their branch tips were already thickening, getting ready to throw off their winter slumber.

The creek between Clara's perch on the flag-stone patio and the early flowers ran heavy and loud, tinged a bit green from last week's snow. And still, she knew the weedy grass and wildflowers would spring up along that waterway before too many more days passed.

A determined metallic *chip, chip* let her know a pair of cardinals had ventured out into the morning with her. They landed on the huge round bird feeder only a few feet away but entirely out of reach to anything without wings. One brilliant red, the other a warm, rich gray, they provided a welcome contrast to the slate of the mountains and the deep blue sky.

She and Shawn had hung the massive glass and metal tower a few years ago, on a metal frame that rotated out over the sharp drop-off along the back of the patio. That and a series of bell-shaped plastic shields turned this feeder into their most successful squirrel-proofing design, much to the delight of what seemed like all the birds within a hundred miles.

The air had a warmer touch this morning than it had since September, back when Clara thought her marriage and her life in this house would be more or less the same after months of cold and quiet.

Not shirtsleeve weather by any means, but warm enough for her to sit outside with the sun on her face, waiting for two new four-legged arrivals.

Wondering whether they'd decide to stay.

Hoping they would.

That they'd bring the exuberance of two young

rescued dogs to the early spring and summer this year, and the years to come.

But too afraid to let that hope take root. Not when the killing frost was still so nearby.

And yet, through her worries, wearing nothing more than jeans, a t-shirt, and a simple black hoodie felt like shedding her heavy winter scales.

As if she was the one with rising sap just under her skin, preparing to burst out with colorful flowers all over her body. Then put on her far lighter garments of green leaves that would feed and comfort her for the long, hot season to come.

Before long, the flamboyant yellow and white daffodils would take over the springtime display, and the heady fragrance of hyacinth would out-compete the delicate scent of awakening green. An amazing variety of birds would join the winter-hardy cardinals, swarming the feeder and demanding more than their fair share of the precious seeds, even though they'd spent months in a warmer place.

But for now, the gentle sights and smells and sounds were enough.

Partly because these earliest days were so fleet-ing, they were the most precious. Worth savoring like all the brief weeks of springtime in her corner of far southwestern Virginia.

Clara had firmly known how lucky she was to live right here her entire life, especially as kinder weather emerged from the deep freeze. Even her great good luck of traveling all over the world had done nothing at all to change how she felt.

All the world around her was slowly coming back to life, and she'd always looked forward to doing the same herself.

For the first forty-one years of her life, at least.

This year, the emerging beauty all around her only inspired images of herself marching back inside her wooden house built right against the side of the mountain. Closing the heavy doors and drawing all the shades down dark and tight.

Never mind the food she'd gotten ready for herself and her arriving guests. The human portion waited wrapped and warm, and kibble and fresh water in stainless steel bowls were set off to the side. Easy enough to take all of it back into the house.

Where she could simply trade in her cup of still-steaming, full-strength coffee for decaf, or perhaps a nice mug of chamomile tea with lots of honey.

Maybe start a fire in the wood stove, or maybe get back into bed and pull her thick pile of blankets up to her chin.

For once in her life, spring could just get on with itself without her marking its arrival.

Because for the first time in more than twenty years, the house was hers, and hers alone.

Shawn was no doubt fighting through the same

melancholy in his own little house not all that far away as distances went in the mountains. Getting settled into an old family home, working out his balance between old and new routines as surely as Clara was.

Probably wondering who would make the phone call today, or whether this would be the day they finally passed a sunrise and sunset without speaking to each other.

Clara's phone weighed heavy in her pocket, just in case.

This gradual separation—the possible slow dissolution of their marriage—wasn't because they didn't love each other, after all.

They were still best friends, and hoped to stay that way no matter what.

Staying *together*, as in living together, had just grown too hard. Too sad.

A reminder of too much shared pain.

The crackle of tires on gravel yanked Clara out of her blue thoughts and reminded her why she was sitting out here in the first place. Not just to enjoy the promising warmth of the morning, though that was indeed a fine reason.

That sound had to be her dear friend Michelle.

And the two dogs who might just stay with Clara and bring a much-needed burst of energy and joy back into the yard, and the house, and her life.

She stood in time to see a mint-green minivan

take the last turn on the long driveway: Michelle's latest rescue vehicle. Someone who worked as hard to help animals and people find their way to each other couldn't possibly drive anything smaller or less practical.

Clara took a quick look around the yard on her way down to open the gate, making sure she had everything as ready as could be for a couple of rambunctious canines.

The shoulder-high fence was still in good repair after years of keeping dogs safe and contained, while giving them plenty of room to run and play. She and Shawn had installed it themselves when they first moved in, wanting to make sure their spoiled city pups wouldn't get themselves hurt or lost on a few hundred acres of land.

The big square garbage cans were properly stowed in their wooden bin, lids secured against raccoons and possums and even the black bears that would soon wake, groggy and famished after months of woozy half-sleep.

They of course had the excuse of being meant to hibernate, unlike people in the midst of a trial separation.

Clara had even moved her car to a new parking spot to make sure no anti-freeze with its sweet and deadly poison waited to tempt dogs. The whole house had gotten a similarly careful inspection.

That was one of the rotten losses she and Shawn

had suffered together over the past couple of years. Losing one dog to old age, then the second to a cruelly fast cancer.

So having a young, healthy pair around shouldn't have felt so...strange after only a few months.

But Clara still paced back and forth in front of the open gate, large enough for a huge pickup truck to get through with no trouble.

What if she forgot something and one of them got sick or hurt?

What if she couldn't keep up with two dogs by herself?

What if the dogs—despite being rescued from an awful situation not that long ago—just didn't like it here?

She shook her head, putting on a smile as Michelle's van rolled through, waving to her friend before pulling the wide gate closed again.

This was a *positive* change, unlike so many that had forced their way into Clara's life lately. One to look forward to.

She just wished Shawn was here to be part of it with her.

And the worst part was his stream of excited questions last night—and the wistful way he wished Clara and the potential new family members well—made her think he wished the same thing.

But neither one of them could quite figure out how to do anything about that.

As soon as Clara walked up the short gravel driveway, Michelle bounded out of the minivan and caught her in a huge, laughing hug.

"I'm so glad to *see* you! Feels like it's been at least ten years."

Clara's return laughter felt as good as the warm sun on her shoulders.

When Michelle stepped back and brushed tears from her cheeks, Clara decided they were all joy from their reunion rather than anything to do with Shawn not being there.

"I'd say more like three months. But that's too long by itself. Got the girls with you?"

The van's door was closed and all the windows open an inch or so, but no sight or sound of the rowdy dogs she'd heard so much about.

Michelle grinned and stepped over to the van's sliding second door. Her dark brown, tightly curled natural hair was pulled back in its usual ponytail, and she wore her normal critter-transport uniform of faded jeans and a brown t-shirt a few shades lighter than her skin.

"They might seem shy at first, but don't let them fool you. Once they sniff you and the yard over and feel like they're safe, they'll burn off every bit of the energy they saved up on the ride over here. Take a few steps back so they can make the decision to check you out."

Clara moved about ten feet away from the van, hoping the dogs didn't take one look at her lanky six-foot frame and decide to jump right back into the van. Not that she'd had trouble making friends with any sort of dog or cat in the past.

But her self-confidence was feeling a little worn thin at the moment.

She nodded at Michelle, who rolled the door back and leaned inside for a few seconds to unbuckle seatbelts and harnesses. The angle of the sun kept Clara from seeing anything, but she finally heard a few curious sniffs.

Michelle backed up and stood to the side herself.

"Okay girlie-girls. Time to take a good look around and see what you think."

Clara only breathed a couple of times, but the wait for a short brown muzzle to peek out of the shadow felt like hours. A compact little pinkish nose wiggled and sniffed like crazy.

Then a sturdy yellowish-brown pit bull jumped out onto the gravels, blinking in the bright sunlight. She had the trademark blocky head and broad shoulders to go with delicate white-tipped feet, but her muscles weren't nearly as big as Clara remembered from the sweet boy she and Shawn had loved for nearly sixteen years.

Right behind her, a huge jet-back Great Dane bounded out, looking around so fast her ears flopped with every motion of her head. She was also thinner than she should be, with too many ribs outlined by the morning light.

"They both have their ears," Clara said, keeping her voice soft but smiling. "They're adorable."

Both dogs looked right at her, with those wonderful floppy ears perked up and curious. Their tails—both a similar slender shape with curls at the end—waved back and forth. Not fearful and tucked under, but not high and confident either.

"Yeah, they're all natural," Michelle said. "That includes not being spayed, but of course the rescue group can help take care of that. I don't think they've had puppies. That was probably what the jackass who had them meant to do, though. That and not much else."

The pit bull raised her nose and touched the Great Dane's much larger one, then she walked toward Clara, sniffing madly the whole time.

"Hey there, pretty girl. Do you know their names?"

"You're looking at Pebbles the Pibble and Great Dana for now. That's what I've been calling them, anyway. No idea what they were named before. But they're lucky enough to be putting that life in their rearview, so whether they actually had any or not, those old names don't matter."

"Pretty Pebbles," Clara said, squatting and holding out one hand. She made sure not to stare right into either dog's eyes. The last thing she wanted to do was intimidate or scare them before they had a chance to settle in. "I'm so very glad to meet you."

Pebbles tilted her head to the side and covered the rest of the distance in a flash, wagging her tail a lot faster. She investigated Clara's hand, sniffing hard several times, blowing out, then repeating.

Finally she kissed Clara's knuckle and looked back at Dana.

Who bounced over in a flurry of flapping ears, long legs, and gigantic grin, without a trace of the caution Pebbles had shown. Thankfully she caught herself before she bowled Clara over. After a snuffling investigation of Clara's face, Dana sneezed, shook herself all over, and set off along the fence line at a quick, ground-eating pace.

Pebbles streaked after her with about ten steps to every two of Dana's.

"Okay, that's fantastic!" Michelle walked over and put her arm around Clara's shoulders. "They'll check the yard out for a while now, so how about you and me sit down in the sun and get ourselves caught up?"

Clara watched the two dogs alternate between walking with their noses to the ground and stopping to inhale the breeze with their heads held high. It wasn't that she didn't want to talk to Michelle, not at all. That was one of the best reasons for this whole hopefully-rescue-a-pair-of-pups operation.

She just didn't love the idea of digging into the slow decline of the last few months, even with a friend she'd known nearly as long as Shawn.

"You'll be happy to know I brought out coffee and a little bit to eat," she finally said. "Assuming you're hungry, of course."

Michelle laughed, which got both dogs turning their way, staring intently. Then they were off and exploring again.

"You know I'm hungry, especially for anything *you* cooked. Any chance you've got sourdough bread tucked away somewhere?"

"You know I do. Toasted, with butter and honey just waiting for you. A few different kinds of cheese to go with it, and a bunch of grapes and cherries. Got some of that food you recommended for the girls, too."

Michelle rubbed her hands and stepped up onto the patio, seating herself in front of a square, tile-topped table. A bundle of blue cloth napkins covered the slices of bread, and a little white crock held butter Clara got from a neighbor a couple of days ago. Two matching pitchers only a few inches tall stood nearby, one full of cream from the same neighbor, another full of honey from the summer before.

Remembering the weekend she and Shawn had spent out on this same patio—laughing and creating a huge mess while making the tile table and several others—brought a watery smile to Clara's face. One she apparently didn't manage to hide.

"I'm not going to pretend I don't wonder what happened between you two." Michelle had already helped herself to the coffee and a splash of cream, and was now spreading a perfectly even layer of yellow butter over a slice of toast. "But I'm not going to push you into telling me anything you don't want to."

Clara slid a piece of extra-sharp cheddar onto her plate before getting her own toast.

Dana bounded onto the patio just then to provide a moment of sweet distraction, with Pebbles hard on her heels. Both girls sniffed the waist-high wooden railing before Pebbles took a couple of crunchy bites of kibble and Dana drank nearly half the water.

They nosed at Michelle and Clara in turn before racing off for more exploration.

"You're one of the few people I'm actually willing to talk to about it," Clara said. "Since you know both of us, and I know you wouldn't take sides even if one of us tried to make you."

Michelle managed to shake her head while taking a big drink of coffee.

"Damn right I wouldn't. You're both my

friends, and neither one of you are assholes. And you don't have to say a word for me to understand that you're both hurting right now."

Clara did a much messier job of adding butter to her still-warm toast, then poured a neat spiral of dark brown honey on top.

"Hurting *was* the trouble, I think. We had a rotten couple of years there, you know? It just felt like that was all we had left between us."

Michelle did know. She'd helped both Clara and Shawn more times than either of them could count. By listening, getting them out of the house together or separately, bringing over a goofy movie or pizza or gin for martinis.

Staying by their sides as much as she could, through burying both of their fathers, their last grandparents, and a painful job loss to go along with saying goodbye to their two sweet pups. Throw all that together with turning forty and mix in a string of bad decisions on both sides, and their shared grief festered and ended up way too toxic.

Until eventually looking at the faces they'd both loved so hard and for so long hurt more than it helped.

Instead of rehashing any of that, or mentioning a single word, Michelle only watched Clara. None of the pitying looks, or worse yet, the angry ones they'd both gotten from their families when they broke the news of the split.

Only a calm regard that somehow managed to make all the scrambled-up parts inside Clara feel a little bit less scratchy and sharp.

"So what do you think of these two goofballs?" Michelle finally said. She whistled and clicked her tongue, and Dana and Pebbles came hurtling from the farthest part of the yard toward the patio. They ran shoulder to shoulder, both of them snarling and flashing their teeth.

And obviously head over heels in love with each other.

This time they both marched straight over to Clara with huge, tongue-lolling grins. She scratched a massive black head and a blocky brown one with equal affection.

"They might look kind of strange together, but they seem like a perfectly matched pair. You said they came from the same place?"

Michelle nodded as she chewed a mouthful of honeyed toast with a generous sprinkle of goat cheese on top.

"The details are a little sketchy, but that's probably for the best. The sheriff called me, said they'd found them locked up inside a house. She never said how long they'd been there. Only that the jerk who left them in there was in jail and likely on the way to prison. All I'll tell you is they were a lot thinner when they came to me a few weeks back."

Clara frowned, then leaned over to shake the bowls full of kibble to get the dogs to pay attention.

She knew exactly how well Michelle watched over the foster pups in her care, and one of the main ways was making sure they got fed. As both dogs started crunching away, Clara decided she didn't want to imagine how they'd looked before Michelle had a chance to feed them up.

Their too-thin frames now were bad enough.

"The saddest part," Michelle went on, "is it was like they didn't really know how to be dogs. Part of it was they didn't have much energy, sure. Barely enough to take themselves outside, especially in cold weather. But then they'd just sit in the yard and look around. Even if I threw a ball for them, or a bird or a squirrel went by. They were curious, but confused. They're getting better, learning more every day. Know the one thing they *always* knew how to do, no matter what?"

Clara only shook her head, even though that ordinary reaction was a lie.

The twenty-one-year-old who'd fallen so hard in love with Shawn might have mostly gotten buried by time and routine, arguments and scars, but she was still somewhere inside.

And she knew.

"Even with all the awful and scary things they've been through," Michelle said, leaning forward and staring into Clara's eyes, "these two girls know they can depend on each other. I've never seen dogs cuddle and snuggle the way Pebbles and Dana do. When I took them to the vet to get checked out, I thought Pebbles was going to cry her little heart out when they took Dana out of the room to do the bloodwork and such. Dana didn't show it as much, because you know as well as I do that pit bulls are little bundles of pure love and emotion. But when they brought Pebbles back, Dana danced around like a hundred-pound fool to see her."

She shook her head and smiled.

"Now don't think they can't fuss and squabble and carry on, because they've been doing that more and more as they get stronger and more confident. But no matter how loud and rough they get, even when I'm convinced they're going to finally get into a real fight instead of playing, they always end up falling asleep together before too much time goes by."

As if to illustrate the point in case Clara wasn't paying attention, Dana washed down her kibble snack with a long drink of water, darkening the tan flagstone with an impressive amount of spillover. She then walked in several tight circles and somehow managed to fold her amazingly long legs into a tight little bundle as she curled up in the sun.

Clara's pang of guilt that she hadn't brought out one of the old dog beds or at least a blanket only lasted until Pebbles finished her own snack. She turned and looked into Clara's eyes for a second before breaking into a broad pibble grin.

After her own post-kibble drink, she stretched herself out with her belly against Dana's back and heaved a long sigh.

Clara couldn't quite hold back her smile, any more than she could quiet the shiver of hope that spread from her heart to her belly and her mind.

"Did you train them to do that? Prove your point for you?"

Michelle held Clara's gaze for a beat before she winked and sat back.

"I don't know what point you're talking about. Unless you mean the obvious one that these girlies are pretty damn comfortable here. Give her a minute, and Pebbles will be snoring like a freight train. Think you can forgive me if I do ask you a question after all?"

"Only because I think these sweethearts are going to be exactly what I needed. And only if you answer one for me first."

Michelle held up her mug in a playful toast.

"Ask away."

"Have you talked to Shawn about all of this yet?"

Michelle finished her coffee and poured more for herself and Clara.

"Not about this, no. Turns out I'm a lot more

comfortable getting into *your* business even if it's his business too. You two still talking on the phone every day?"

Clara nodded as she swirled a little honey into her coffee, then a little cream.

"So far. He's excited to hear more about me meeting the dogs, so I'll probably call him in a little while."

"He talks about you as much as he did when you two were together, Clara. I should probably keep my mouth shut here, but between that and the phone calls, I gotta think there's still something left."

Instead of jumping right in with explanations about how a trial separation worked—which both she and Shawn had done too many times with their own families—Clara closed her eyes.

She didn't see his hard mouth and furious eyes, or hear his anguished voice or feel the desperation of his hug the night they'd said goodbye. Right before he drove away and they both spent so many nights alone.

All the things that had haunted her when she listened to the silent house and tried not to count the minutes until the sun came up.

A tensed-up, protective part of herself relaxed its grip for the first time in months. Just enough to let her breathe into the part that hurt the most.

The part that loved the most, too.

She opened her eyes to see Dana and Pebbles

shift their napping positions, ending up with Dana's huge head draped over Pebbles' side. Neither one showing any signs of fear after all they'd been through, even in a place they'd never been before.

Because they were together.

"There might be something left," she said, reaching across the table to squeeze Michelle's hand. "Maybe I'll invite him over to meet the girls later."

Michelle squeezed back.

"That sounds like a great idea for all four of you. I can't tell you how many times I've faced up to how much smarter my dogs are than I could ever be."

At a buzz in Clara's pocket, Michelle, Pebbles, and Dana all looked at her with their heads tilted to the side.

And the whisper of hope in Clara's belly came through in her voice when she answered without looking at the phone's display.

"Hey sweetie. Yeah, they're here, and Michelle. Want to come over and see how much you love them at first sight? And I'd like to see you myself."

KARI KILGORE

AUTHOR OF PUNGENT JUSTICE AND WHAT BREAKS A MAN

Popcorn and the

Precious Pebbles Antique Shop

*For everyone who loves wandering
in a great antique shop*

and to the always helpful shop cats who welcome us

CHAPTER 1

AMBER STEVENSON HAD NEVER SEEN another little mountain community with as many antique stores as her hometown. And all the different ones in Pebble Creek, Virginia, somehow managed to be interesting in their own unique way.

That was one of the best things about coming home from college to visit. Knowing the wonderful stores would be there, mixed with the excitement of seeing all the new things they'd gotten in stock during her time away.

The one near the athletic fields for the high school specialized in all kinds of sports. They had a world-class collection of baseball cards to go along with old wool uniforms from the days when all the coal mines had their own teams. Tiny gloves by modern standards shared wall space with thin leather football helmets that were downright scary to contemplate.

Over by the big hiking, horse, and bicycle trail was a shop packed full of everything necessary to set out for a long day in the great outdoors. *If* you happened to be outfitting yourself for sometime before World War I broke out all the way up to the summer when men first walked on the moon. Ancient saddles and bridles, bikes with a front wheel almost as tall as the riders, and fine examples of huge canvas tents that were not at all backpack friendly.

Amber had to admit she loved the one tucked in with the best restaurants in town, even though she wasn't quite sure what to do with those cooking supplies any more than current offerings from the age of smartphones. But wandering the aisles stocked with gorgeous blue and red glassware older than her grandparents sent her on waves of wistful nostalgia. The plain white coffee cups and ordinary glass tumblers in her apartment suffered greatly in comparison.

She did admit contemplating hand-crank mixers, genuine ice-block-on-top iceboxes, and a vast, coal-black iron cooking stove left her thankful for her microwave and ability to drive to the grocery store or order takeout.

Her favorite antique shop out of more than a dozen she made sure to visit even for a long weekend was tucked away in a residential area not far from her parents' house. In fact, it was inside a house not all that different from the one she'd grown up in.

A big two-story brick rambler built when Model-Ts were the height of automotive technology and indoor plumbing was quite the luxury outside of town, Precious Pebbles Antiques didn't have a clear theme like so many of the other shops did.

But Amber knew she wasn't the only one who caught the excitement of a new discovery there more than anywhere else in town as soon as she walked through the door.

She got a surprise of the unexpected kind when she strolled down the tree-lined street toward the shop, enjoying a delightfully crisp and breezy October fall-break day.

The earthy aroma of a wood fire somewhere nearby fled from her mind, along with the brilliant blue sky and leaves just beginning to take on their autumn finery.

Because something strange sat in the big gorgeous lawn in front of Precious Pebbles.

Rather than some sort of vintage lawn furniture or spectacular display of chrysanthemums scattered across the perfectly trimmed grass, a chest-high wooden sign sat right in the middle. Words that made no sense at all in Amber's mind were carved into the wood, and painted a warm, cheery yellow that popped with the rich brown background.

Come On In and Meet the New Owner!

Amber nearly tripped on her own Birkenstocks when she saw that, even though the sidewalk was flat and level and swept so clean it sparkled in the sun.

The McDaniels had owned Precious Pebbles since before she was born. Since before her *parents* were born. Some of Amber's earliest memories were sitting on the broad wooden checkout counter, unable to take her eyes off the numbers flashing inside the top of the huge brass cash register that had been ancient back then.

She'd understood all those years ago that Larry and Pamela McDaniels were...well, *old* themselves. But she'd somehow managed to convince herself they were eternal, and never revisited that belief.

Amber squared her shoulders and shook off her surprise. She wasn't about to give up before she even walked inside and introduced herself.

And while it made her feel a bit disloyal to the McDaniels, she was more than curious enough about this new owner that going back to her parents' house unequipped with all the information (and gossip) she could get simply wasn't an option.

Everything seemed as it should be, at first.

The same huge copper cowbell—closer to the size of a cooking pot than the tiny things she'd seen musicians use—rang out a musical chime over the front door. The McDaniels told her years ago that it came from a trip they'd taken to Switzerland sometime in the 1970s.

The room she stood in had the same sort of random and wonderful collection of antique chairs she always felt compelled to test out on every visit.

Here an angular, low chair with polished wooden arms and flat leather cushions. There an amazing egg-shaped chair, gleaming white outside and startling red velvet inside. Against the wall—which was newly covered with every imaginable variety of picture frame with samples of brilliant flowered wallpaper inside—a tall-backed sofa covered with images of pheasants of all things.

Beside every sit-able surface, a table that may or may not be from the same era waited. Heavy oak two-level end tables, an odd blue ceramic table shaped like an elephant dressed for a festival, and a sturdy bookshelf covered with glued-on marbles and seashells.

Each surface held its own sort of riches. Everything from strange statues and figurines to elaborately decorated tea services to a collection of little metal radios not much bigger than Amber's cell phone.

She caught a whiff of strong coffee cutting through the comforting smells of books and well-cared for fabrics and general age, which wasn't too far off from the usual tea aroma. And the other rooms she could see looked pretty much the same as well.

So she should still be able to browse among vintage lamps, tablecloths, and shoes to her heart's content. Soaking in the comfort of her own personal homecoming ritual of wandering to see if a new old find begged to go home with her.

The fact that she rarely bought anything didn't matter. It was the routine of immersing herself in the past that made all the difference.

But Amber wouldn't truly settle in until she got an idea who these new people were, exactly where the McDaniels were, and how much one of those fabulous egg chairs cost these days.

She'd just drawn breath to call out a greeting when something rather noisy in the vicinity of her right foot beat her to it.

A comfortably padded cat with white shaggy hair and black spots sat gazing up at her with huge orange eyes, blinking once, then letting out a second meow like a rusty screen door swinging open.

"Hello right back to you."

Amber leaned down and patted the cat's head, smiling when said kitty responded by raising off its front feet and pushing against her hand. Then followed up by walking under her hand to extend the petting all the way down its silky back to the tip of a remarkably bushy tail.

"You know how to get exactly what you want, huh? I could take a lesson."

The cat ground out another meow and circled back around for a repeat.

"I'm guessing you're in charge around here now, since the McDaniels never had a cat, much less one as friendly as you. Any chance your people are nearby to say to a neighbor?"

The cat wove itself between her ankles, brushing against her jeans and pausing to sniff at her bare toes. It let out one more meow—this one loud and long enough that Amber wondered if the poor thing would end up with a sore throat—then flipped that showy tail high and streaked off down the hallway.

Amber giggled. "Was it the way I assumed you're *not* running the place by yourself? Or just a comment on my lack of a pedicure?"

She shrugged, wondering if anyone else in Pebble Creek was less likely to have polished and painted anything than her. She couldn't even say that's what several years of working as a river guide down in North Carolina while she finished up her masters in history did for her, since a couple of women and at least one man she worked with managed to keep their fingernails *and* toenails immaculate.

Nothing for it, really, except to perch in that gorgeous egg chair and see if it actually would spin in a circle before exploring further to see if the friendly, rusty-voiced cat really was the new owner.

She'd only gotten in a few good spins before another surprise had her smacking her sandaled feet down to bring the chair to a halt.

One rotation, and all she'd seen was the rest of the groovy potential seating finds going by in slow motion.

On the next, a striking woman stood in the hallway, leaning against the wall, arms crossed.

A woman wearing the same blue-jean-casual look Amber's sharp-dresser of a father still occasionally tried to convince her to set aside once in a while.

And Mystery Woman's threadbare jeans and a perfectly faded blue Johnson City Cardinals t-shirt could have come straight out of Amber's own closet. At the sight of the gronky cat sitting primly in the hallway beside her, Amber couldn't stop a grin that was likely about seven different kinds of goofy from taking over her face.

Thankfully Mystery Woman was smiling too.

"Sorry about that," Amber said, pushing herself out of the wonderfully comfortable chair. "I've always wanted to sit in one of these, and of course I got busted before I could get any real speed going. I'm guessing you belong to the sociable kitty?"

"That's probably the best way to put it. Popcorn here takes her customer service job quite seriously.

And no worries on the chair. I did exactly the same thing when it came in. It goes pretty fast as long as you can keep from getting dizzy."

Popcorn—the cat who sounded like she needed an oil change—slow-blinked at Amber, then looked up at Mystery Woman and commented with another of her rough, adorable meows.

"Popcorn, huh," Amber said. "I'd ask where that name came from, but I should probably tell you mine first. I'm Amber Foster. I saw Popcorn's sign outside and figured I should stop by."

"Kirstie Brinson, Popcorn's business manager. She's been keeping me busy with inventory like you wouldn't believe. She's great at checking underneath everything and sniffing out the truly hidden treasures, but can't seem to manage handwriting or typing. Good to meet you, Amber."

Kirstie held out her hand, and Amber couldn't quite fight back a giggle at her perfectly manicured pink fingernails. At least her father would have approved of that much.

Kirstie raised one eyebrow at the giggle, but didn't seem the least bit offended.

"Did you... I mean did *Popcorn* take over from the McDaniels?" Amber said. "I halfway grew up in here from what my parents tell me, which was apparently the most interesting when I was learning to walk and could out-toddle whoever was watching me and knock things over. Before that, Pamela would plop me down on the counter while my mother browsed, and Larry would fuss about how I was going to fall off and crack my skull."

Now Kirstie laughed, the sound of it as smooth and rich as hot chocolate on a snowy day.

"They didn't mention their side-hustle watching neighborhood babies, but that sounds about right. I'll have to see if they'll share their marketing tips. They're fine, by the way. A couple of folks who've dropped by seem to think I did something nefarious to get them to sell. They're down in Atlanta spoiling their great-grandchildren purely rotten, but no reports on how their skulls are doing so far. Looks like yours held up pretty well."

Amber thumped her own head with her knuckles, glad about a thousand times over that she'd decided to stroll over this way. She hadn't met anyone this easy to talk to for ages.

"My parents are always telling me how hard-headed I am, so I might have had a natural advantage. How long have you and Popcorn been here?"

Kirstie leaned down to scoop Popcorn up in her arms, and got a gravel-throated comment and a remarkably loud rumbling purr in return.

"We made the arrangements back in the spring, but the McDaniels decided to keep it pretty quiet. I think they wanted to enjoy all the summer festivals around here without the drama, or distracting everyone, you know? This town has more festivals than antique shops, and that's saying something. They finally had their big send-off party and headed south toward the end of August. Did you say you're studying history?"

Kirstie laughed again and shook her head, blushing just like Amber often did when she realized she'd been talking nonstop.

"And I'm sorry, I'm being terribly rude, which Popcorn tells me won't win me any new friends or keep my establishment's loyal customers. Can I get you a cup of coffee, or tea or water? It's been quiet today, but I keep the kettle hot just like the McDaniels told me to."

Amber stepped forward to scratch Popcorn's fluffy head. First behind her black ear, then her white one.

"You're following a quality time-honored tradition there. I think Pamela gave me my first sip of cream and sugar with a little coffee mixed in and started my favorite life-long habit. I don't add much of anything if the coffee is good these days, but I'd love a cup."

CHAPTER 2

KIRSTIE COULDN'T HELP IMAGINING a tiny, adorable Amber toddling full-speed around the shop. Or else perched apple-cheeked and smiling on the walnut-brown polished surface of the counter between them now, maybe with her shiny brunette hair caught in two pigtails.

Envisioning the room from that stinking-cute little girl's perspective was even more fun.

The checkout counter itself was nearly four feet wide, and more than six feet long. The behemoth came up past Kirstie's waist, so it had to have been gigantic to a toddler's eyes. Of course the shelves built into the customer-facing side would have presented an endless array of amusements and temptations.

Right now it was full of books she and Popcorn had retrieved from all over the store and the converted garage out back that was stuffed full of not-yet-displayed gems. The old gold-spined Little Golden books sat comfortably beside early editions of Nancy Drew and the Hardy Boys, and all of them kept company with a selection of huge coffee table books from the days when every coffee table included an ashtray.

The rest of this cozy room, too small to hold anything as big as the coveted egg chair, was full of more odd things Kirstie had rescued on her first wander through the shop. She'd cleared off all the shelves and displays and started from scratch.

Except for the gorgeous brass cash register, still in the same place of honor on one side of the counter. She'd replaced the McDaniels' adding machine with an iPad, sure. The sleek white stand holding it was so jarring compared to everything else that she'd finally covered it with an orphaned bit of vintage paisley upholstery fabric. Besides looking amazing, the pattern was so thick and textural that she wasn't the only one who couldn't resist touching it.

There was a lot to be said for the tools of less-stressful modern accounting, but that didn't mean they shouldn't have style.

The cash register still stood proud and solid—along with a rotating selection of antique vases full of fresh, fragrant flowers—ready to welcome everything she moved in before she re-opened the doors for her open house on the first of September.

A somewhat creepy cat clock with moving eyes and tail. A stunning Barbie-doll-sized wardrobe, complete with mirrors, outfits for every occasion on tiny coat hangers, and little drawers full of matching shoes and hats. Surprisingly pretty blue and green glass insulators rescued from some upgrade of the power lines or another, looking like stacks of rounded sparkling doughnuts.

Her only rule on that first pass had been picking out things that were off to the side, hard to see for someone casually strolling by. Dusty from not being handled recently helped, even though the McDaniels had kept such a full shop remarkably clean.

Popcorn truly had led the way on those expeditions, with an unerring ability to discover the most amazing thing in each room.

Handmade or store-bought, necessity or trinket, every item already inside or waiting in the storage barn had been important to someone once upon a time.

And Kirstie (and Popcorn) thought it was worth creating the chance for these once-valued things to find a new home rather than ending up in a landfill somewhere.

A person had desired it or needed it, enough to part with money that may have been hard to come by at the time. And they'd used or read or displayed what they'd bought, taking good enough care of it to leave it ready for a new treasured life.

Kirstie was more than half-convinced the reason the McDaniels had chosen her—out of everyone who'd responded to their extremely quiet and low-key feelers about selling the store—was that she understood the difference between junk and something of value.

She had the same knack of sorting through everything from an old house to a storage unit to a cardboard box and knowing what was worth that second (or third or fourth) chance.

Not that contemplating any of that was worth ignoring her own chance to get to know the fascinating woman in front of her.

Amber had the irresistible air of someone who didn't have the slightest clue how smart they were. And an old Pebble Creek High t-shirt, black jeans, and open-toed Birkenstocks on a cool day put her firmly in the comfort-before-fashion crowd where Kirstie felt most at home.

But the honest truth was Kirstie had been intrigued since she'd caught the joyful, delighted expression on Amber's face when she was spinning around in the chair, very much like that toddler might have done.

"So tell me about your t-shirt," Amber said, making it clear Kirstie wasn't the only one who was curious. "Was it yours, or did it come from some-one's collection?"

Kirstie grinned and took a sip of her black coffee.

"Would you believe no one else has said a word about it? And I wear this or another one like it all the time. One of my aunties lived over in Johnson City, and she was a lifelong Cardinals fan. Took us to games every time we came back from Pennsylvania for a visit. So I bucked the trend and grew up not liking either the Pirates or the Phillies."

Popcorn took that moment to make her hop, skip, and jump way from floor, to footstool, to counter. She ignored Kirstie altogether and waltzed back and forth in front of Amber, rubbing her cheeks shamelessly against Amber's hands.

"You sound like my family in Michigan and Georgia," Amber said. "They took their team loyalty with them too, for generations now. Odds are non-zero that we were both at a game in Johnson City some summer or other."

Amber sipped her coffee, which she did indeed take straight up, and concentrated on petting Popcorn. Who promptly stretched out on her belly with her legs straight out behind her.

The exact same pose she employed when she wanted Kirstie to pay attention to some neglected, half-hidden item in the shop or barn. They'd proven worth bringing out front and putting on display, every time.

Friendly as Popcorn usually was with strangers, Kirstie had never seen her get anywhere near this comfortable with someone she'd just met.

"My goodness, she must get her daily yoga in or something," Amber said, continuing to lavish the silly kitty with affection. And carefully not looking at Kirstie. "Anyway, you asked me about studying history, which I am. Wrapping up the classroom part of a master's degree this winter. Which I am *not* sure what in the world to do with. I'll probably end up laboring away in some museum somewhere, since I don't much want to teach."

"Now *that* I understand. No one expected my years of studying interior design to lead me to owning an antique shop, least of all me. I didn't mind the work, and I was pretty good at it for years. I've been getting a few jobs on the side here, so it's coming in handy and helps pay the bills. But I'm just more...I don't know, comfortable with the things in here. Everything in here speaks to me of a different time, a different place. A world I catch a glimpse of that I never get with something brand new. I love things that already have some miles on them."

She blinked, then stared down into her own cloudy cup of coffee. Feeling like she was the one with a lot of miles that had somehow loosened up her hold on her own mouth. She doubted Amber had come in to hear a bunch of late-thirties career-change angst when Kirstie hadn't even started making her own choices about work.

But when she risked a glance up, Amber grinned instead of checking her watch or looking away.

"That's the *very* thing I love about history. And why I kept going with it even though I knew I didn't want to teach. All those stories, like reading some kind of massive book of fiction, except they're true. Well, as close to true as some of them can be from so long ago. It feels like the more I learn, the more I get to live at least an echo of all those lives. I never get tired of researching and finding out more. But I've never figured out how to explain that until just now, or what I can do with it."

Amber paused to take a deep, slow breath.

Kirstie felt her own chest rising and falling in sympathy, remembering her own conflicted feelings when she'd decided to step away from her own expected career and buy this shop.

"Who knows?" Amber said. "Maybe spending so much time here is what set me on that path to begin with. Maybe the only place I *could* say all that out loud for the first time is right here."

Kirstie couldn't get a word to come out of her mouth. She'd never heard anyone explain it like that, and hit so close to how she'd felt when she first walked into this shop.

All those lives...

And all that excitement about a bunch of stuff so many people took for granted. From a different angle, yes.

But she had the feeling Amber would understand exactly what the leap of buying the shop and changing her life was all about.

Kirstie jumped when the cowbell over the front door rang, torn between relief and irritation at the interruption.

Amber laughed and brushed behind one ear with a smile.

Maybe she'd felt that instant friendship connection as clearly as Kirstie had.

"Just dropping your mail," a cheerful voice called out, and a faint thump sounded from the front room. "Anything else going out?"

Kirstie cleared her throat. "It's all there," she called out. "Thanks, Peggy."

Popcorn picked that moment to let loose with a strident, drawn-out meow in her life-long smoker voice, turning her head to stare pointedly at Kirstie. It was surely imaginary, but the look seemed to demand she *do* something, *say* something to this nice lady who was so patient with all the petting.

Now!

The words got themselves organized and out of her mouth before her thoughts ever got a start.

"Every try your hand at researching antiques?" she said. "Trying to figure out where things came from? Popcorn is the real pro when it comes to pointing out things I should pay attention to, but she's about as good at explaining what she finds as she is at accounting."

Amber frowned for a second, but it looked more like concentration than annoyance.

"You mean for valuation?"

"That's part of it, but I meant more for letting people know what's here. Or helping people find what they're looking for, or what they've got. Maybe deciding whether they want to sell or not. From what people have told me since I got here, none of the shops in town are all that good at that part of the job, strange as it sounds."

She tapped her fingernails against the glass surface of the iPad, lurking behind its paisley fabric disguise.

"Most of them do a quick internet search and call it good. Your neighbors have noticed, and I'm sure tourists have too. The folks who were good at that side of the business all seem to have retired or moved on or passed on. That search gives a value in cold, hard cash, or zeros and ones to get even more impersonal. A date on the calendar, maybe. But it leaves out *why* these things mattered then. And to me, that's why they matter now."

She waved one hand, taking in the room and the rest of the shop.

Hoping she was making sense, and even more, hoping Amber was actually interested, even if she wasn't quite sure what her idea was yet.

"Much as I love everything here," Kirstie said, "I'm barely a beginner when it comes to knowing what it all *is*. And the storage barn out back is even worse. I don't think the McDaniels knew half of what they had stashed away in there. Maybe you can help me and Popcorn start to figure it all out."

CHAPTER 3

Amber continued to pet the friendliest, most flexible cat she'd ever met, attempting to wrangle her jumbled thoughts into some kind of working order.

It wasn't only that she'd spilled her guts about her impending career worries, which she'd never admitted to anyone else. She'd barely started facing that unpleasant reality for herself.

It was more that Kirstie hadn't looked at her like she was crazy or selfish or lazy, or determined to be some kind of eternal graduate student with no plans of ever making a living.

All things Amber had wondered about herself over the last few months.

She hadn't launched into the well-meaning lecture Amber had heard too many times from relatives, random unwelcome commenters, and academic advisors about how she had to make sure all that education *paid off* in some undefined, socially acceptable way.

In fact, Kirstie had admitted she'd not only turned away from her own studied-for career, but also understood why Amber might keep studying with no clear destination in mind.

How rare was it that someone she'd just met *got* her like that?

Probably at least as rare as feeling comfortable enough with a complete stranger to talk about things like this in the first place.

A smart, interesting stranger who'd just suggested...a job?

"Do you mean as a consultant or something like that?" Amber said.

Kirstie smiled and tilted her head to one side.

"I don't know. Maybe? This is new to me, and I know you're still wrapped up with school. We could start off that way, see how working together suits us. Then if we're both interested in more, go from there. But consulting doesn't mean volunteer, so we'll have to talk about the money part too. If you're interested, that is."

Amber finished her coffee, deliberately taking her chance to stall out the immediate "Of *course* I'll take the job!" response ricocheting through her mind. Because wasn't that kind of speak-without-thinking thing every bit as bad as not having any kind of plan at all?

Even though she'd been chasing herself in circles inside her mind, trying to find something that felt like a good fit for her, that sounded worthwhile and satisfying?

Working in this beloved shop might be all that and an outstanding use of all her education at the same time.

"I'm interested," she finally said. "As long as Popcorn approves. Sounds to me like we'd be working pretty closely, so I don't want to step on any toe-beans. And maybe let me in on how she got her name someday."

Kirstie laughed, and Popcorn sat up, adding her own sweet sandpapery commentary.

"From what I've seen so far, you two will get along just fine. As long as you don't mind taking inventory advice from a cat. She hasn't steered me wrong so far, and I don't think she has today. As far as the name, when she curls up the right way, her fur looks like a great big bowl of fresh popcorn. Silly but true."

Amber looked around the cozy room, the scene of so many of her earliest memories, and the source of her favorite stories about herself from even further back.

When it came to completing circles, she might

have strolled her way into a wonderful chance to do just that.

"I think Popcorn might turn out to be my best teacher yet."

I hope you enjoyed meeting all the sweet critters in Four-Legged Heroes. My real-life critters approve with cuddles and kisses!

For more, turn the page or join me at www.KariKilgore.com/Collections.

ALSO BY KARI KILGORE

I hope you enjoyed reading the stories in *Four-Legged Heroes* as much as I enjoyed writing them.

For more stories where speculative elements are either slight or not there at all, head over to www.KariKilgore.com/ContemporaryFiction.

If you're craving more adventures from the Appalachian Mountains, and in many genres, head over to www.KariKilgore.com/TalesFromAppalachia.

For fantasy of many kinds, visit www.KariKilgore.com/Fantasy.

If you're in a romantic mood, you'll find more at www.KariKilgore.com/Romance.

Check out more of my fiction, including almost every genre, and be first to hear about release dates, Kickstarters and other fun projects, and exclusive e-book and print editions at www.KariKilgore.com.

Collections:

Fantastic Shorts: Volume 1

Fantastic Shorts: Volume 2

Fantastic Shorts: Volume 3

Escape into Romance

Stepping Out of Reality

Facing Down Extraordinary

Hacking Cybercrime

Investigations Beyond Belief

Passages in the Real World

Fantastic Side Trips

A Kaleidoscope of Cat Tales

A Tapestry of Holiday Tales

Aunties Among Us

Anthologies *with Jason A. Adams*:

Partners in Romance

Shadows Mountain Deep

Uncommon Holidays

Partnership in Crime

Dispatches from the Galaxy:

Restricted Species

The Becalmed

Plurapod Pathogen

The Changes Cascade

Near Future Forward (with Jason A. Adams)

Dispatches from the Galaxy: A Space Opera Novella Trio

Dangerous Days on a Pleasure Planet

Novels:

Until Death

The Dream Thief

Hand Me Downs

Protecting Her Own

The Coffee Bomb and the Corporate Spy

The Great Gold Record Heist

Novellas:

Legacy of the Land

In the Pines

Fantastic Women: A Dark Fantasy Novella Trio

DNA Never Lies

The Box of Possibilities

Murder at the Fabulous Feline Emporium

Team Building Revenge

Storms of Future Past:

Dreaming the Storm

Joining the Storm

Into the Storm

Fighting the Storm

Storms of the Heart

Storms of Future Past Omnibus

Voices Through Time:

Songs in the Mountain

Secrets in the Land

Sorrows in the Earth

Walking the Ghosts

The Odd Society:

Independent by Means of Magic

Protected by Means of Magic

ABOUT KARI

Kari Kilgore's wanderlust and imagination lead her all over the world on grand adventures. Her heart and family bring her home to her native Appalachian Mountains of Virginia. From that solid base, she and her husband Jason A. Adams bring those adventures to life in fiction.

More than her fair share of wonderful pets—including fish, hamsters, guinea pigs, birds, mice, cats, and dogs over the years—bring her plenty of warmth, love, and inspiration.

Kari writes contemporary fiction, fantasy, mystery, romance, and science fiction, and she's happiest when she surprises herself. She lives with Jason, various house critters, and wildlife they're better off not knowing more about.

The Confidential Adventure Club

For Kari's exclusive free After The End stories and deleted scenes, discounts, early releases, adorable pet photos, Kickstarters and other fun projects, Spiral Publishing Exclusive Edition print

books and e-books, and a whole lot more not available anywhere else, join us in The Club.

Hope to see you there!

www.KariKilgore.com
www.SpiralPublishing.net
www.ConfidentialAdventureClub.com

BB bookbub.com/authors/Kari-Kilgore

a amazon.com/author/KariKilgore

g goodreads.com/KariKilgore

f facebook.com/Kari.Kilgore.1

ADDITIONAL COPYRIGHT INFORMATION